DESIGN for MURDER

Frederic Arnold Kummer

DESIGN for MURDER

Frederic Arnold Kummer

COACHWHIP PUBLICATIONS

Greenville, Ohio

Design for Murder, by Frederic Arnold Kummer
© 2023 Coachwhip Publications edition

First published 1936
Frederic Arnold Kummer, 1873-1943
CoachwhipBooks.com

ISBN 1-61646-547-6
ISBN-13 978-1-61646-547-6

I

Stephen Ransom's first impression of Halfway House was a delightful one.

A wainscoted hall, with two grizzled Scotch deerhounds licking his fingers. The long, low morning room . . . a horizontal sweep of gayly colored chintz. Many standing figures, crossing it in dark vertical lines. Beyond them a doorway, its opening almost filled by a huge cluster of hydrangeas. Vivid blue blossoms as big as muskmelons, against a fainter turquoise sky. Hydrangeas in April. The marble vase that held them, with its ring of dancing *bacchantes*, might have come from an ancient Roman garden. Brilliant sunlight gave it a warm, mellow *patina*, like old gold. The simple, stark beauty of the arrangement left him breathless; the next moment he was greeting Mrs. Kirby.

"Good of you to ask me," he murmured.

She laughed nervously, shaking her head; it made her jewelry rattle. Too much jewelry, Steve thought, for an informal luncheon. For any luncheon. Priceless earrings, a pearl necklace, bracelets. They seemed to clash with the blue hydrangeas, the graceful vase. A matter of taste. Her eyes, however, were simple and rather plaintive.

"I saw your play," she said. "The detective one. Liked it a lot. You know I'm interested in the theatre. We'll talk, later. Now you'll want a drink. Edward!" She beckoned a liveried servant carrying a tray. "And to meet some of these people. Mrs. Conover . . . Judge Tyson" . . . her nod embraced a couple near by . . . "this is Mr. Ransom; he writes plays. And . . . oh . . . Count de Zara," she added as a dark, immensely broad man joined the group. "Yes, Edward." Smiling, she moved away, rather quickly, Steve thought.

He shook hands, juggling his cocktail.

"We've been talking about murders," Mrs. Conover laughed. She was small and blonde and suavely *soignée,* like a fragile figurine at de Zara's elbow; he could have crushed her in one of his powerful hands. "Judge Tyson, you know, is an expert on the subject; he's sent dozens of murderers to the gallows."

"Dear me!" The judge, plump and smiling as a well-fed bishop, regarded Mrs. Conover with a merry eye. "Is that nice? Before luncheon, too. Bad for the appetite. Anyway, I've retired from the bench."

"But you *did* say there had been a murder in this house," Mrs. Conover persisted, shivering gracefully.

"That is not good!" De Zara brushed back his coarse, polished hair. "In my country the people think that murders, like goats and . . . and chickens, breed . . ."

"How horrible!" Mrs. Conover shivered again, as though she enjoyed it. "Have you a little murderer in your home? Ugh!"

The judge finished his cocktail.

"At the time I spoke of," he said, glancing about the long, low room, "this was not a home . . ."

"What was it, then?" Steve asked, puzzled.

"A tavern . . . an inn. No doubt the Father of his Country slept here more than once . . . although with whom, if anyone," the judge added, chuckling, "history does not say. It was called 'The Half Way House,' I suppose, because of its location between Alexandria and some point in Maryland . . . Bladensburg, perhaps. Washington, the city, of course hadn't been built then. I imagine this was used as a tap-room . . ."

"But the murder?" Mrs. Conover insisted. The judge shook his head, frowning.

"Like a puppy with a root. Or a cat with a mouse. Well, I've always maintained that women are more bloodthirsty than men. The proprietor, I understand, finding his wife in the arms of an admirer, promptly strangled her."

"How inconsiderate!" Mrs. Conover laughed, wrinkling her small, impudent nose. "He should have strangled the admirer."

"Perhaps the gentleman escaped by the window, the garden." Judge Tyson gazed over the blue hydrangeas to the sweep of lawn beyond. "There is a double row of box trees outside at least fifteen feet high. A perfect lover's lane. Not so tall, a century ago, of course, but tall enough to serve the purpose. English box, you know, grows only an inch or so a year"

"Really." Count de Zara moved away, covering a yawn. "If you excuse". . . he joined a tall, handsome girl standing near the door.

"Russian?" Steve inquired, gazing after him.

"No. Dalmatian, I believe." Mrs. Conover's lips curled wickedly. "Anyway, some kind of a spotty breed. That's Jean Kirby he's after. I'll bet the senator doesn't like it. I know his wife doesn't; she's told me so. Furious! These Continental business men certainly do know their Bradstreet."

"I have never," Steve said, "seen such a chest and shoulders. He has Primo Carnera beat . . ."

"Probably got them pulling on ropes or something. Just one of the Volga Boatmen boys. Or is it Jugo-Slavian? I don't believe all the titles I hear. Why . . . hello."

Mrs. Conover turned as a slender, distinguished looking man joined them. "Dr. Badouine, you know Judge Tyson, don't you? And Mr. Ransom; he writes plays, although I'm ashamed to say," she added with a small laugh, "I've never seen any of them."

"Not surprising," Steve grinned. "They don't run beyond Opus Number 1, so far. Although I've finished a second; am trying right now to get someone to produce it."

"Better talk to Mrs. Kirby; she's mad about the stage. I hope it's a detective play. We've just been talking about murders, doctor. That sort of thing ought to be right in your line . . ."

"Really?" Dr. Badouine's large brown eyes flashed with humor; he smiled at the judge. "Luckily we physicians can make mistakes without being hung for it . . ."

"But . . . I didn't mean that, darling." Mrs. Conover laid a tender hand on the doctor's arm. "I was speaking of detecting crimes, not committing them. Dr. Badouine," she explained to Steve, "is a psycho-analyst. He doesn't finish you off with knives or drugs."

"I've always thought," Steve said, "that a good psychiatrist might do a pretty fine job, as a detective. Getting at motives, all that . . ."

The doctor laughed; the suggestion did not seem to displease him.

"A psychiatrist," he said, "really *is* a detective. He spends his time tracking down inhibitions, complexes, dragging them out into the open. Helping his patients to get rid of them. Such mental quirks are apt to be dangerous killers . . . if not of the body, then of the mind. I've spent weeks, months, sometimes, on their trail." He turned to Mrs. Conover, who still had her hand on his arm. "I promised to show you the hyacinths; they should be in bloom, now."

"Charming woman," the judge said, as the two moved off.
"A widow?" Steve asked.

"Not officially. Her husband, I believe, prefers New York and the Racquet Club as a steady diet; Mrs. Conover likes Washington, and its, er . . . attractions . . . better."

Steve glanced about the room. About twenty guests in all, he thought. Laughing, chattering. He caught bits of conversation, fragments. "Not a chance, I tell you . . . the Supreme Court settled that!" "Huh! Nine old men! Ought to change our national motto to read 'In the Supreme Court we Trust!' Ridiculous!" . . . "Certainly the Abyssinians aren't Christians!" . . . "Is that so? Then all I can say is there are going to be a lot of disappointed Ethiopians hanging around the Pearly Gates!" . . . "Yes, I prefer the lighter shade; I hear Mrs. Roosevelt uses it." . . . "They tell me Senator Kirby expects to land a cabinet job, if his party wins the next election" . . . "You mean Lawrence Dane, the actor? Yes, he's here. Over by the door talking to Jean Kirby. And that big foreigner who looks like a gorilla. De Zaza, or something" . . . "Sure . . . I'll speak to the Secretary about it at once."

Judge Tyson followed Steve's glance.

"Mrs. Kirby," he said, "likes unusual people; always tries to get together an interesting crowd. Actors, politicians, titled foreigners . . . writers," he added, smiling.

"Which is Senator Kirby?" Steve said; "I've never met him."

"Over there by the fireplace. The tall, bony man that looks like a Westerner. Which he is. The little fellow with the sandy hair is his lawyer, Luke Reed. The lobbyist. Smart as a fox. Looks like one, too. Come along and I'll introduce you."

The room was choked with a verbal clatter. As they came near the two men Steve heard Luke Reed's voice, razor-sharp, cutting through.

"Don't be a fool, Tom! If you do, it'll mean your ruin! I'm telling you!" Senator Kirby, over the heads of the crowd was staring harshly at his wife.

The Judge coughed. A tentative cough.

"Hello, Tom! How are you, Luke!" he said. "Shake hands with Mr. Ransom, one of our budding young playwrights."

The two men, Steve thought, were displeased by the interruption.

"Still very much in the bud," he laughed. "You have a wonderful house, Senator. I appreciate being asked to it. If you don't mind I'll have a look around. See you later." He strolled off, paused near the doorway to pat one of the deer-hounds. A slim, well-shaped girl with dark, shining hair and very direct grey-blue eyes came up to him; her knitted silk suit fitted her supple body like the skin of an apple.

"Are you Mr. Ransom?" she said.

"Guilty." Steve straightened up, smiling.

"I'm Ann Vickery. Mrs. Kirby says you're to take me in to lunch. Out, rather." She nodded toward a glassed-in terrace covered with small tables. "Five minutes, yet; we may as well sit down." She sank on one of the chintz-covered sofas. "If you want a cocktail wave for it. I don't, just now. They tell me you live in Baltimore."

"Yes," Steve said, scratching the dog's muzzle. "And you?"

"New York. I'm down here for a few days giving estimates on doing over Mrs. Kirby's personal suite . . . I'm an interior decorator. Do you like the house?"

"Swell . . . what I've seen of it. This room. And especially those flowers in the doorway. A perfect touch. Exquisite!"

"Yes." Ann Vickery nodded. "I thought they'd look well there. Had them brought in from the conservatory this morning. The vase was down by the lily-pond. I suppose you've seen the garden?"

"Not yet. Maybe you'll show it to me, after lunch. Senator Kirby must have plenty of jack, to run a place like this."

"No. It's his wife's. Cigarette money. I don't mean that the way it sounds," Miss Vickery added, with a wide smile. "Tobacco money. Millions. Poor woman."

"Most people wouldn't figure it a hardship exactly."

"I don't mean her money. She isn't well. Neurotic. Mentally upset. Dr. Badouine is treating her. You met him?"

"Yes. Handsome young physician . . . went out to look at the hyacinths with a snappy blonde named Mrs. Conover. I've got them straight. What's Mrs. Kirby upset about?"

"Her daughter, Jean. That tall, smoldering-eyed girl in black. She wants to marry Count de Zara. Mother objects."

"Why? Anything wrong with de Zara? I'd figure him a professional strong man . . . magnificent, from the neck down . . ."

"Nothing wrong that I know of. They say his title's quite genuine. Maybe she doesn't like the man . . ."

"Do you?"

"I've only met him twice . . . and I mustn't gossip. But I don't care much for foreigners . . . especially the fortune-hunting kind. However, I may be wrong. He seems quite sincere."

Steve glanced about the room.

"It's always a bit confusing," he said, "meeting a lot of strangers. I've got Mrs. Kirby ticked off. And her daughter Jean. And Dr. Badouine and Mrs. Conover. And Count de Zara. Judge Tyson is the plump little lawyer who looks like Santa Claus. And the bony old buzzard by the fireplace is Senator Kirby . . . with his legal man of all work, Luke Reed. That's the bunch, as far as I've gone . . ."

"The slim, smooth-faced man in the doorway," Ann Vickery said, "talking to Jean Kirby and the Count, is an actor, named Lawrence Dane. Doing local stock."

"Friend of Mrs. Kirby?"

"I believe so. But I'm practically a stranger here. Let's talk about something else."

"All right." Steve grinned. "How about me? I'm no modest violet. I suppose Mrs. Kirby told you what I do for a living?"

"She said you wrote plays."

"Right. At least, that's my delusion. I get quite a kick out of it. Looking for material. What would you think of this house, as a setting for a play? Your blue hydrangeas are a perfect touch. A mystery play. I hear there's already been one murder, in this room."

"Fair enough, for a setting. But why a murder? Another murder, I mean. There would have to be a motive . . ."

"What about Mrs. Kirby? Simply dripping with priceless jewels. I suppose they're real."

"Oh, yes. She told me the other day there was no point in having jewelry if you couldn't wear it. No doubt her things are insured. That rope of pearls she has on, I understand, is worth a quarter of a million . . ."

"And you talk about motive! What more do you want? As for the murderer, take me, for instance. Poor but ambitious playwright. More or less broke. The lady, having seen my first opus, is good enough to ask me to lunch. Doesn't know me from the town pump. I may be a desperate criminal . . ."

"You don't look it," Miss Vickery grinned.

"The big shots never do."

"I see. And where do I figure, in this drama?"

"Oh . . . you're my little pal. 'Moll,' I believe, is the proper underworld term . . . the *mot juste*. Sent down here by me to look the ground over in advance . . . otherwise 'case the job.' You've just informed me how much the lady's pearls are worth. When I whistle under your bedroom window . . . 'give you the office' . . . you trip downstairs in your pyjamas, let me in, and the deed is done. After that, Paris . . . or would you prefer the Argentine?"

"I don't care for the role," Ann Vickery said. "My instincts are naturally moral. Can't you think of something more elevating?"

"No. I like this plot. Strong love interest. That always makes a big hit, with the public. Hero and his girl-friend in the shadow of the guillotine! Noose, to be exact; they still hang 'em, down here. We'd beat the rap, in the last act, of course, by pinning the crime on the butler. That's always safe." He glanced up as one of the liveried servants bent over to announce that luncheon was served.

"Hope he didn't hear you," Ann Vickery said, laughing.

"If he did," Steve grinned, "your reputation is shot; tomorrow you'll probably find yourself in the hoosegow. Well . . . that's what comes of associating with playwrights. A disreputable bunch! Where is this luncheon party? I'm hungry enough to eat a dish of spinach."

II

Ann Vickery climbed out of the tremendous tub and swirled a bath towel about her waist like a sarong.

Undoubtedly the Malays had the right idea, she thought; a one-piece costume made life simpler. Still, carrying that argument to its logical conclusion, why wear anything at all? At least there would be an agreeable saving in laundry bills.

She grinned at her smooth, shapely body in the mirror. Some people, she thought, might go in for nudism without causing the public to laugh itself to death. There were others whose cascading stomachs and overhanging hips made the idea seem almost obscene.

Why did people have mirror-lined bathrooms anyway? Narcissism, that was the technical term for it. A form of vanity, no doubt. Although what pleasure anyone could get out of that sort of thing was beyond her.

She put on her pyjamas, went to the window. Time to go to bed, time at least, for poor but honest working girls. She grinned again, at that, surveying her surroundings. The marble bathtub was almost big enough to swim in. Silver plumbing. Gold-plated doorknobs. Just another way of showing off, of course, by people with more money than taste. Like children, with toys. Not the senator, perhaps; politics was his passion. Still, that might be a way of showing off, too.

The garden, however, was perfect. Age, and a good landscape artist had seen to that. She could just make out the dark box hedge, with the antique stone bench at the end of it, the blue lily-pond. Blue in the daytime, only a flash of silver, now, under the moon. She would have enjoyed sitting there, at this moment, with someone she liked very much. Someone with loose, russet-leather hair like Stephen Ransom's. And eyes that knew how to laugh. Life was so damnably serious most of the time. Fighting for money. Not money for gold-plated doorknobs. For living. The kind of living a man and woman with taste would want.

She frowned at the absurd bed, which suggested a stage setting for Madame Du Barry. Silk sheets. Why should anyone want to sleep between silk when they could get good honest linen? Mrs. Kirby must have put her in the royal suite.

She had just kicked off her mules when she heard the voice. It came, she thought, from the morning room below. A woman's voice, high, excited. Ann could distinguish only three or four words. "I know!" Or was it "No . . . no!" Followed by "The nail!" or "That nail!" The exclamation, while meaningless to her, was somehow alarming.

For a moment she stood at the bedside, her body tense. The voice had almost certainly been that of her hostess, Mrs. Kirby, and there had been both surprise and fear in it. She waited, expecting something more to follow that excited and meaningless cry.

What followed was the radio, suddenly turned on. An adenoidal tenor, gargling a cheap love-song. There was a radio in the room below, Ann knew, but this seemed scarcely the sort of program that Mrs. Kirby would select. Still, it was difficult to tell, with women in their forties. Lonely, sex-starved women; if nothing else, her three-days stay in the house had told her that the senator and his wife were not exactly lovebirds.

Above the whining of the tenor Ann heard another sound. The deep, rich chime of a clock. She counted the strokes. Twelve. Strange. She had not supposed it so late; her watch, lying on the bed table, still marked a quarter before the hour. The clock, of course, might well be wrong; she had noticed the tall mahogany case, the brass dial, the day before, and thought it a museum piece. These antiques were not always to be relied upon she knew.

For a time she waited, sitting on the bed, uncertain whether to put out the lights, go to sleep, or undertake some sort of an investigation. True, there seemed nothing in particular to investigate, nothing, at least, that concerned her. In any case, there were plenty of servants in the house, although at this hour they would doubtless be in bed. She turned the light switch, darkening the room except for the small glow of a reading lamp. Recollections of Mr. Stephen Ransom's comedy-drama, with herself as the hard-boiled heroine, drove her, smiling, to the window. According to the scenario he should shortly be whistling beneath, waiting for her to come downstairs and let him in. As she glanced toward the garden, she thought she saw a furtive dark figure moving against the deeper black of the box trees.

Ann Vickery was not the sort of woman to be easily panicked. Life, although it had not left her hard, had made her efficient, like a well-tuned airplane motor, an adding machine. What she had heard and seen did not add up right. The high, strained voice, the sticky crooning of the radio, the clock, striking incorrectly, the figure silhouetted against the boxwood hedge, no one of these things, taken separately, seemed adequate cause for alarm; Mrs. Kirby might well have been talking to some late caller in the room below: she had difficulty in sleeping, stayed up until all hours. Her voice was normally rather high, shrill; a nervous voice. Old clocks were often out of order. Tastes, in radio programs, were apt to differ. As for the dark figure—perhaps it was customary, in this unfamiliar household, for visitors to come and go by way of the garden. Each circumstance, taken by itself, admitted of reasonable explanation; together they made up a total that Ann Vickery's logical mind rejected. She slipped her bare feet into the mules, pulled a dressing gown about her shoulders, went into the hall.

The suite which had been given her was in the east wing of the house; the part of it that had once been the original tavern. Ann thought of that, as she tiptoed along the dimly lit corridor; thought of the century-old murder of which Stephen Ransom had told her. Perhaps the jealous husband had crept down this very hall, as she was creeping now, to surprise his wife and her lover in the room below.

Each wing had its own separate staircase. The broad, polished steps creaked a little as Ann felt her way down them, holding on to the smooth mahogany rail. Somewhere below, toward the main part of the house a lamp was burning, but the faint light from it did little more than intensify the shadows. She reached the newel post, stopped. Except for the sound of the radio the house was singularly still. The program had changed. Someone was playing a guitar, now, singing a Spanish ditty; it sounded less offensive than the buttery love-song had done.

At her right, the door of the morning room was closed. Ann went up to it, knocked. Not loudly; she felt like an intruder, wondered, when she met Mrs. Kirby, just what she should say.

There was no response to her faint knocking. Probably the noise of the radio had drowned it out. Acting on impulse, she turned the knob of the door, pushed it wide.

The room was brilliantly illuminated. Facing her a French window stood open. The flagstone tiles of the terrace outside, under the amber light, were like squares of copper. To her right, in the doorway of the solarium, the cluster of hydrangea blossoms showed now only a splotch of muddy indigo; they needed sunshine, for their vivid blue. To the left, toward the fireplace, was a writing desk; Chippendale, an old piece.

Mrs. Kirby was sitting at it. She sat very still. Her head, bent forward, rested on a square of tan blotting paper. A tall man stood over her, gazing down at the back of her neck. Without being told, Ann knew that Mrs. Kirby was dead.

The man turned to face her. She had realized that it was Stephen Ransom, even before his shoulders moved. During luncheon she had liked his quick, whimsical smile, the sparkle of laughter in his eyes. There was no laughter in them now, nor was he smiling.

"Miss Vickery!" he exclaimed. "Mrs. Kirby has been murdered I'm afraid. You'd better rouse the family. Have them call a doctor, the police!"

He spoke softly, trying to control his excitement, but Ann saw that his hands were trembling.

III

Steve Ransom hadn't cared much for the play—a local stock-company tryouts. The construction was poor, he thought. Too much running in and out of doors. Unexplained entrances and exits. It wasn't so easy, he knew from experience, to get one's characters logically on and off stage. Just dragging them around by the back of the neck was amateurish. Still, the dialogue had been modern, snappy; the piece might get a run on Broadway.

He knew one of the authors slightly, thought of looking him up. Then he decided not to. It was always a strain, to talk to another writer about his work. Frankness might be construed as envy. Plain goose-grease, smeared on, he left for back-slapping hypocrites. And silence, while safe, was often the most deadly criticism of all.

There was Lawrence Dane, of course. The tall, good-looking actor he had met at Mrs. Kirby's luncheon. Unfortunately, the authors had seen fit to kill him off for their second act climax; by now he was probably miles away, enjoying his after-theatre supper.

Thoughts of supper reminded Steve that he was hungry himself. He got into his car, drove down Pennsylvania Avenue. Since he had elected to eat alone, any place would do. He went into an almost empty tiled restaurant, ordered scrambled eggs and bacon, coffee.

21

The girl who waited on him seemed ill. Her cheeks were flushed, under heavy, too brilliant eyes. Steve noticed, as she scrawled the items on a pad that her fingers were quivering.

"Feel badly, sister?" he asked.

"Uh-uh. Flu, I guess." The girl pressed her side, coughing. "That be all?"

"Yes." Steve nodded. "What time do you get off?"

"Twelve. It won't be long now."

Steve glanced down at his wrist watch. Eleven twenty. He took a dollar bill from his pocket, pressed it into the girl's clammy fingers.

"Here," he said. "Settle the damage and keep the change for carfare. Then go on home. Tell 'em you're not fit for work. If you don't you're likely to be laid up with pneumonia. Now beat it."

The waitress went away, whispering thanks. Steve devoured his eggs, thinking of Mrs. Kirby. They had talked, very briefly, after luncheon, about his new play; the demands of her other guests had prevented a longer conversation. He had not come to Washington with any idea of interesting her financially in a stage production, but she had asked him about costs, made him write the figures down on a sheet of paper. The woman, he thought, was eager for something to occupy her mind and energies, something which would provide excitement, afford her an outlet for her emotions. He grinned, at that; she'd get excitement enough, backing a show. And why not put some of her over-large income into a theatrical venture? It was a better gamble than many stocks, a more interesting one than roulette, or horseracing—you got more fun for your money. Sig Krantz had liked his new comedy immensely, but complained about production costs. Too many sets, too big a cast, he thought. Being what he was, Sig considered one set and six people the ideal American drama, unless he could cut the speaking parts down to four or less. With Mrs. Kirby's backing, the play could be put on properly and the excitement of it might lift the poor woman out of her mental doldrums. She had certainly seemed ill. Perhaps it was difficult, being the wife of a prominent senator. Perhaps politics, its constant demands, left Kirby little time for his wife. Perhaps there was something else—vaguely in his mind Steve remembered some nebulous gossip involving the Senator and a certain unknown woman . . . a widow. Was it Mrs. Conover, he wondered?

He finished supper, went out to his car. The hour's drive home would be pleasant enough on this mild spring evening, with clear roads and a moon. He thought of the girl he had met, the attractive interior decorator . . . what was her name . . . Vickery . . . Ann Vickery. Good-looking, and intelligent. Something smart, streamlined about her. That was New York, of course . . . a New York training. He wondered if she had been born there . . . thought the chances against it. Most New Yorkers hailed from the sticks; from her manner of speaking he figured her as down east . . . not too far down. Rhode Island . . . Connecticut. An interesting girl. Good mind . . . swell figure . . . he'd like to see her again.

The Kirby's place was swell, too . . . just the sort of place he'd like to own himself, if he had plenty of money. Rambling old house, every line of it suggesting large, leisurely comfort. Like a well-tailored suit, of costly material but comfortably worn. Even a little baggy at the knees perhaps. The old-fashioned garden would be attractive, he thought, by moonlight. Like a stage setting. Not much out of his way, to drive by and look at it.

The view of the house from the avenue was disappointing because of the trees at its front. The side street, however, not much more than a lane at the east of the garden, gave him what he wanted. He stopped the car alongside a field-stone wall; spring had covered it with a tracery of Virginia creeper, deep bronze now, although by day it would be a tender green.

Over the wall, the east wing of the house was surprisingly close. A room on the ground floor showed a row of long windows, amber oblongs cut in the somber brickwork. Beyond a wide terrace, the double row of boxwood trees showed a deeper, more vivid black than the surrounding shadows. There was no movement in the still picture, no sound, except the dim drone of a radio from inside the lighted room. The same long, low room, Steve reflected, in which he had been during the early afternoon—the room in which the innkeeper's too-affectionate wife had met her untimely fate.

Smiling, Steve reconstructed the scene. A similar spring evening, no doubt: such affairs blossomed with the crocuses. The agitated lover, doing a hasty nose-dive through one of the windows. Not French windows, then; those were probably a later embellishment. An escape through the shrubbery.

Steve paused, frowning. One of the tall windows had been pushed open. A figure in black . . . a long black coat, or cloak . . . flitted across the terrace like a hasty shadow and instantly melted away, became one with all the other vague shadows that crowded the garden.

For a moment or two Steve sat still, peering uncertainly into the gloom. Had the figure he glimpsed been that of a man or a woman? He could not tell, although the swirl of the long, dark coat had seemed feminine to him, rather than masculine, the suggestion of a hat more like a toque than any headgear a man would be likely to wear.

Now that the window was open he could distinguish the sound of the radio much more clearly, could almost hear the words of the song. Common sense told him there was no reason why anyone, either a man or a woman, should not have left the house, gone into the garden, and yet, why emerge with such suspicious rapidity? Why make such a swift and dramatic exit, leaving only a well-lit room, a blaring radio behind? There should, he felt, be something more. Some evidence of movement behind the amber shades of those tall windows. If a visitor had left, the one so suddenly opened should be closed again. At approximately midnight, even the most trusting of householders did not leave their windows open to a rude and unscrupulous world.

As a dramatist, a writer of plays, Steve Ransom had made a study of exits. The one he had just witnessed suggested very strongly a hurried flight . . . the villain making his escape from a vacant stage, leaving tragedy behind. If so, it was too late, now, for pursuit of that fleeing figure. But not too late to investigate the reason for his, or her, sudden departure. Even at the risk of being himself taken for a midnight burglar.

Laughing a little at his imagined fears, Steve Ransom jumped from his car, vaulted the low stone wall. The grass of the lawn was smooth and soft with the softness of spring; his feet made no sound on it. Beyond was a flagstone terrace, on which the tall windows faced.

Because of their draping curtains it was impossible to see through them. Hurrying a little, Steve reached the one that stood open, stepped into the room.

IV

Ever afterward, Ann Vickery remembered the horror of that first moment. The dead woman, at the desk, the long, bright room, too bright, now, with its flood of light, its gay chintz, the ordeal she knew to be facing her—all seemed suddenly and equally horrible. Except, perhaps, the tall figure of Steve Ransom. Even in that tragic moment she was aware of his good looks, the careless smartness of his grey flannel suit, the grave distress in his eyes, the way in which his red-brown hair grew down on his forehead in an attractive peak. Somehow, these inconsiderable details seemed all she had to hold on to, in a world that had begun to reel.

"I think the family . . . the others . . . are out," she said unsteadily. "The senator spoke of a political meeting, at dinner; thought he would be late. Jean Kirby is with her fiancé. The servants are in bed." She met Steve's grave look with a question. "How did you get in?"

"The window was open." He glanced behind him, one eyebrow quizzically raised. Ann remembered their mock mystery-drama then; according to its scenario *she* was to have come down and opened it.

"You might call Dr. Badouine," she went on. "He's a psycho-analyst, but I don't know anyone else. And if

. . . if the poor woman is dead, I suppose it doesn't make much difference. There's the phone." She pointed to a table against the wall.

"Yes." Steve picked up the telephone directory, began to search for a number. The radio, its Spanish tinkling ended, burst into full orchestra; a gust of dance music . . . jazz. Ann moved to stop it.

"You won't be able to hear—" she said.

"Don't!" Steve warned. He held the small, bright telephone instrument between fingers wrapped in a handkerchief. "Don't touch anything. Also, the radio may help to check the time." He spoke into the transmitter.

The time? Ann glanced at the tall clock. Five minutes to twelve. That agreed with her watch now. Yet she had heard it chime the hour, ten minutes before. Somebody must have moved the hands back. She stared at Steve Ransom, wondering.

"Dr. Badouine is expected at any minute," he said. "I've left word for him to come at once." He called another number . . . presently spoke again. "This is Senator Kirby's residence. Halfway House. I'm reporting a murder. Mrs. Kirby. I don't know. A friend. Neither of them. Yes . . . a Miss Vickery; she's visiting here. Yes . . . Dr. Badouine. They're asleep. All right . . . we won't. I understand."

"Well?" Ann watched him put down the telephone.

"We're to stay here. In this room. Not to touch anything. Not to call the servants. Just wait, until the police arrive." He glanced toward the desk.

"What makes you so certain Mrs. Kirby has been . . . murdered?" Ann asked, pulling the dressing gown tighter about her waist.

Steve went to the body.

"That," he said, indicating a point on the dead woman's neck.

A small, red spot, like a puncture, was barely visible near the base of her skull. But for the fact that the surrounding hair was thin, and ash blonde, the wound would scarcely have been noticed, at least not by a casual observer; there was no blood.

"Oh!" Ann murmured, shuddering.

"Looks as if somebody had driven a sharp, round instrument into the base of her brain."

"Horrible." Ann felt a little sick, fought against it.

"Like the Spanish *garrote,*" Steve went on, palpably trying to divert her with conversation. "Official Castilian equivalent of the electric chair. An iron collar with a spike in it; you turn a wheel and the spike is forced through the spinal cord. Quick, and not painful, they say; shouldn't care to try it myself."

Ann was still staring, white-lipped, at the small round wound.

"It *might* have been a nail!" she whispered.

"Nail?" What gave you *that* idea? Rather inconvenient sort of a weapon; you'd need to carry a hammer around as well. The only nail murder I ever heard of is in the Bible. Lady named Jael got rid of a gent called Sisera by driving a spike into his dome; she used a mallet. Perfect, for a little jingle. There was a young lady named Jael, who bumped off a guy with a nail . . ."

"Don't," Ann said slowly. "I know you're trying to take my mind off this thing, but there's something I must tell you. Before I came downstairs I heard Mrs. Kirby cry out, as though she had been frightened. She said, 'The nail!' or 'That nail!' I'm not quite sure which."

Steve stared at her, puzzled.

"That's queer!" he muttered. "Darned queer! According to the Bible story, it's a female weapon. And just before I came in here I saw somebody leave by the window . . . in a hurry. Couldn't be sure, then, whether it was a man or a woman. Now I am. Look at that." He pointed to one of Mrs. Kirby's hands, lying clenched on the desk-top.

Ann bent over. Between the dead woman's fingers were several long strands of dark hair.

"A woman's, of course," she whispered. "Her pearls are gone, too!"

"Pearls?" Steve glanced up, incredulous. "You don't mean to tell me she had the damned things on all evening?"

"She certainly did have when I saw her last, about ten o'clock. She was sitting here reading. And waiting for somebody . . ."

"How do you know she was?"

"I heard her tell Edward, the butler, so. Said she was expecting a caller, very late . . . that he needn't wait up . . ."

"H . . . m." Steve, staring down at the blue and tan Indian rug beneath the desk, bent over, frowning. "The string must have been broken in the struggle, then, because here's one of the pearls on the floor. Better not touch it. Or those scraps of paper; I promised the police not to mess up any clues. There certainly seems to be plenty of them; I suppose you've noticed the wall safe. Over the mantelpiece." He crossed the room.

Ann followed him. The ancient fireplace had been fitted with an elaborate Caen-stone mantel. In the chimney-breast above, a Della Robbia plaque, a brilliant bit of enameled terra cotta apparently fixed in the plaster, had been swung aside on invisible hinges, revealing the polished steel dial of a safe beneath.

"An ordinary thief wouldn't have known how to turn that thing back," Steve said. "Wouldn't have known there was a safe behind it. Somebody's been burning papers, too; you can see a few scorched pieces, at the edge of that smoldering backlog. Somebody who was in a hurry, or they'd have done a better job. How long was it, Miss Vickery, after you heard Mrs. Kirby cry out, before you came downstairs?"

"Six or eight minutes, I suppose. And she didn't exactly cry out. Not, I mean, in the way anyone would call for help. First I heard her say about the nail. Then the radio went on . . ."

"Immediately?"

"Yes. A sickly love song called 'Nobody, Honey, But You.' I thought it a queer selection, for a woman like Mrs. Kirby. Then the clock struck . . ."

"You mean this clock. Struck what?"

"Twelve."

"But it wasn't twelve—isn't yet, for that matter."

"I know. I looked at my watch. I thought the clock was wrong."

"It's O.K. now by my time."

"And mine. Of course the striking mechanism could be out of order. Or the hands may have been turned forward until it struck, then put back again. We ought to know in a few minutes, because in that case it will strike one, next." Ann suddenly became conscious of her bare ankles, her mules. "I suppose I should have come down sooner but I didn't suspect . . . at first. And I'd been taking a bath."

"Funny mixup," Steve said. "Too many clues. If you ask me, I'd say some of them had been planted."

"Planted?"

"Sure. To make things more difficult, for the police. Why should an ordinary jewel thief be burning letters . . . papers? And those strands of hair in Mrs. Kirby's fingers. Maybe they were put there, to throw suspicion on somebody."

"On me, maybe." Ann laughed, not happily. "Well, the color *is* about right."

"Don't forget you found *me* . . . bending over the body." Steve waved to a couch. "Suppose we sit down and talk this thing over."

"Just where we were sitting this afternoon," Ann said, falling back against the pillows, "when I told you how much Mrs. Kirby's pearls were worth!"

"And I planned, with your help," Steve added gloomily, "a swell little robbery and murder! Ha! Just about the way it actually occurred!" He jerked his long body upright against the back of the sofa. "Do you realize, little one, that we may be in a rather tough spot? All my fault, too. Well, pal," he put out his hand, "it looks like a case for co-operation."

Ann gripped his lean, hard fingers.

"Moll, I believe, is the proper term," she said gravely. "And I suppose you mean we've got to hang together."

"Thank God," Steve exclaimed, with sudden enthusiasm, "for a woman with a sense of humor! Oh, gallows, where is thy sting?"

He held her hand firmly . . . was still holding it when the police car roared into the driveway.

V

Inspector John Duveen, Assistant Superintendent in command of the Detective Bureau, Washington police, pressed the doorbell at Halfway House, frowning. Contrary to his usual habit, he was in a state of indecision.

On the one hand he felt a little sorry that the Major had been called out of town and was thus prevented from taking active charge of the case. The importance of the persons involved promised to make it an affair of unusual difficulties.

Not that the Inspector objected to difficulties, in the ordinary sense of the word. As an able and conscientious officer he rather welcomed them. But he knew, from experience, that when great wealth and political position were both involved, obstacles were sometimes thrown up against which even the most able and conscientious worker might readily bark his shins, or, as the Inspector mentally put it, mixing metaphors a little, burn his fingers. Senator Kirby was a man of great influence, not likely to forgive any mistakes.

On the other hand, the fact that the Chief *had* been called away left the Inspector with that joy which comes to every man, when required to carry on in the absence of his superior. He was not looking for an alibi; all he wanted was a fair fight, with no favors given, or asked, especially asked. But he would have to be careful of pitfalls.

The door of the house was not at once opened, in spite of his continuous ringing. Ann Vickery and Steve Ransom, bolt upright on the sofa in the morning room, heard the distant bell but made no effort to answer it; their orders had been to stay where they were, until the police arrived. It was left to Edward, the butler, hurrying downstairs in slippers, bathrobe and a very bad temper, to open the front door.

The three men in citizens' clothes who stood beyond it were three men to him and nothing more. His frown suggested that to ring a gentleman's doorbell at midnight was something not done, in polite circles.

"Well?" he demanded, holding the door slightly ajar.

"Senator Kirby in?" The Inspector's voice was snappy.

"I think not." Edward's manner still remained on the lofty side.

"Don't you know?"

"I haven't heard his car return."

"How about Mrs. Kirby?" Duveen was studying his man.

"Mrs. Kirby was in the morning room when I last saw her. About eleven o'clock. Now I imagine she has retired for the night."

The Inspector had prolonged the conversation for his own purposes. Seeing the door begin to swing inhospitably toward him he pushed it open, almost upsetting Edward in the process.

"Police!" he said grimly. "Show us the morning room! Come along, boys!"

The butler, in a daze, tottered down the passage toward the east wing, muttering.

"Here, sir," he said, opening a door. The first thing he saw was Mrs. Kirby, sitting at the desk and the grim

stillness of her figure appalled him. "Madam . . . I . . .
Oh, my God!" he muttered, and fell, babbling, against the
doorframe.

The Inspector went past him, glanced about the room.
In it he saw the body, the wall safe, the open French window, the two figures standing beside the couch. Perhaps
even other, more minute details were recorded automati-
cally by his subconscious mind.

"All right, boys!" he said. "Hurry up with your pictures,
Carey; the Doc'll be along any minute now." He swung to
Ann and Steve. "I'm Inspector Duveen, Detective Bureau.
Who are you?"

"This lady is Miss Vickery," Steve said. "A guest in the
house. I'm Stephen Ransom. The one who called the police."

"What are you doing here? Guest too?"

"No. I happened to be passing the house, saw someone
run out of that window, thought I'd better investigate . . ."

"So you came in. What did you find?"

"Mrs. Kirby. Sitting there. Dead."

"How'd you know she was dead?"

"I felt her pulse."

"Did, eh? What else?"

"Nothing. Then Miss Vickery joined me."

"Why?" The Inspector turned to Ann.

"I heard noises, ran downstairs, found Mr. Ransom
here. Asked him to telephone."

"How come you didn't do it yourself? Or call some of
the family? Instead of leaving it to a strange man?"

"I knew everyone was out. And Mr. Ransom isn't a
strange man; I'd met him before."

"Oh! You had?" The Inspector's eyes narrowed a little.
"Where?"

"Here. At luncheon. Today."

"I see." Inspector Duveen paused for a moment; he
was trying to reconcile this statement with Steve's alleged

quite accidental arrival on the scene. "What noises did you hear, miss?"

"I heard the radio. And the clock strike twelve. But principally I heard Mrs. Kirby call out something about a nail."

"A nail? I don't get you." The Inspector's eyes were questioning.

"She said, in a loud voice, 'The nail!' or 'That nail!' I'm not sure which. I don't know what she meant."

"Was there anybody with her?"

"I suppose so; she wouldn't have been talking to herself. And I thought I saw someone moving in the shadows, but I have no idea who it was."

"Why not your friend here?" Duveen glanced at Steve. "You found him in the room when you came down."

Ann had no answer for that, attempted none. It was Edward who spoke. Weakly, because of the horror still upon him.

"Perhaps I should say, sir," he mumbled, "that just before eleven Mrs. Kirby told me she was expecting a caller, sir, but as it might be late she'd let them in herself, and I could go on up . . ."

"Let *them* in? What do you mean by them?"

"That was the word Mrs. Kirby used, sir. I got the . . . ah . . . impression that she did not wish to disclose her visitor's name."

"Then you don't know whether it was a man or a woman?"

"Oh, yes, begging your pardon, I do, sir. It was a woman. My room on the third floor happens to command an excellent view of the entrance way, sir. And as I chanced to be looking out, and the moon was quite bright . . ."

"I see. You were spying. Well . . . who was it? Do you know?"

"I do not, sir. Just a woman. Rather a tall woman, I thought, although that may have been because she wore a long, dark coat. I could not see her face . . ."

"The person I saw run out of that window," Steve said, "also wore a long, dark coat. I thought it was a woman, too."

"When was that? What time?" the Inspector asked.

"A few minutes before twelve. Five or six."

"This young lady," Duveen snapped, "says she heard the clock strike twelve before she came downstairs."

"I did," Ann agreed, "but it struck wrong. Fifteen minutes wrong. That was another reason I came."

"Seems to be O.K. now." Duveen glanced at the clock.

"The hands must have been turned forward, then back again. I'm sure of that, because at midnight, just before you came, it struck one. Didn't it?" She looked at Steve.

"Correct." He nodded.

"Then, miss, if it first struck soon after you heard Mrs. Kirby speak, she must have been killed at about a quarter to twelve. Is that right?"

"Yes. You can check the time because at the same moment I heard someone singing a song called 'Nobody, Honey, But You,' over the radio; we haven't touched it since; they signed off at twelve o'clock."

"H . . . m." The inspector nodded. "That ought to fix the time of the murder pretty close." He looked at Steve. "Easy enough, young fellow, for you to have monkeyed with the clock, before this lady came downstairs."

"Right. Only I didn't. If I had, I'd have turned the hands back, not forward. Tried to show the murder took place before I got here, instead of afterwards. The only thing I did, beside call the police, was telephone Dr. Badouine."

"Badouine? Who's he?"

"Mrs. Kirby's physician. One of them, at least. The only one we knew. A psychiatrist. Shouldn't have known that only we met him here today, at lunch. They told me at his house he was expected any minute and would come right along. I knew a doctor couldn't help but it seemed the proper thing to get one. Left word Mrs. Kirby had met with an accident."

The Inspector frowned, pulling at his clipped red moustache.

"Suppose you tell me, young fellow," he asked, "how you happened to be hanging around the house tonight just when the murder occurred?"

"It's simple enough. I live in Baltimore. Drove over in my car today for Mrs. Kirby's luncheon. Later, as long as I was in town, I thought I'd see a show. A new one, a try-out, I wanted to look over. Write a little myself—plays. Well, after the play I had something to eat, then decided to drive by here on my way home and take a look at the garden by moonlight."

"This house isn't on the way to Baltimore."

"It's not much out. And I wasn't in a hurry."

"Where were you at a quarter to twelve?"

"I don't know, exactly. Couldn't have been much before that when I left the restaurant."

"What restaurant?"

"I don't know that, either. A beanery on Pennsylvania Avenue; I didn't notice the name. I can find it, I think. There was a waitress . . ." Steve hesitated, stopped.

"You mean she'd remember when you paid your check and left?"

"No. As a matter of fact the girl was pretty sick. Had a rotten cold. So I gave her the money in advance, told her to go on home."

"Then you can't prove when you left the restaurant."

"No." Steve agreed, thoroughly uncomfortable. "Not unless somebody else remembers me."

"And you might have been hanging around here any time, after the theatre let out, say at eleven."

"That's right. Only I wasn't."

The butler, still shivering beside the doorframe, stepped forward, looking at Steve with pale, troubled eyes.

"There is something I should perhaps say, sir," he muttered. "Although it may not be important."

"Well?" The Inspector wheeled about.

"I've just remembered that one of the second men, name of Parsons, was talking, after luncheon, in my pantry. You know how the servants in a house often do say a word or two now and then, sir, about the guests. Well, Parsons told me he heard a gentleman . . . this gentleman, I think it was," he blinked at Steve, "talking to Miss Vickery about Mrs. Kirby's pearls."

"Pearls?" the Inspector demanded.

"Yes, sir. Her necklace of pink pearls. She was wearing it this evening, but just at present . . ." he nodded significantly toward the body.

One of the plainclothes men came forward, cupping something in his hand.

"Just found this, Chief, on the floor near the desk."

The Inspector looked at the pearl; his body stiffened.

"Go on," he said to Edward.

"Yes, sir." The butler licked dry licks. "According to Parsons, sir, he heard the lady tell the gentleman . . . they were sitting just here on the couch, sir . . . that the string was worth a quarter of a million. And after that the gentleman told the lady she was to come downstairs and open the window for him, and when the deed was done they were to run away to . . . to the Argentine, I think Parsons said. I did not attach much importance to the matter at the time, sir, thinking they were probably joking, but . . ."

The room was significantly still. Steve Ransom laughed, over the heavy silence.

"That's true," he said. "I was amusing Miss Vickery by outlining an entirely mythical mystery play."

Inspector Duveen, judging from his expression, failed to find the matter amusing. He glanced through the open French window, noticed with approval the uniformed officer on the terrace outside. The man who had exhibited the pearl drew him toward the desk, pointed to the dark strands of hair caught between the dead woman's fingers. For a moment they whispered together; Ann Vickery saw, from their glances, that they were discussing her own shining, blue-black locks.

"Get this Parsons," Duveen snapped, nodding to Edward.

"Look here!" Steve took a step forward, towering over the Inspector a good six inches. "This is all hooey. I've told you the truth. So has Miss Vickery. We don't know anything about Mrs. Kirby's murder. Or the pearls. If you want to search me . . ."

"You'll be searched, don't worry!"

The Inspector's voice was glacial. He turned to examine some scraps of paper one of his men had gathered from the floor. "Just now I'd like you to write down a few words for me." He produced a notebook, a fountain pen. "Here! Use this blank page."

"What shall I write?" Steve asked belligerently. "And why?"

"Never mind why. Put down, 'It will cost you' . . . then some figures . . . say twenty-five thousand dollars. That's all."

Steve bent over a corner of the desk, scribbling. The request seemed meaningless to him. The Inspector, however, apparently thought otherwise; he took the notebook Steve handed him, held it alongside the scrap of paper in his fingers. For a moment he stood comparing the two, then laid both on the desk.

"Did you write that?" His lean forefinger indicated some words scrawled upon the torn bit of paper.

Steve stared, astounded. In his own handwriting, were the identical words, "It will cost you," followed by a dollar mark and some partly torn figures. Then remembrance came, swift, if not exactly reassuring.

"Yes," he said. "When I was in this room, just after luncheon today. Mrs. Kirby thought of putting money in a play of mine. She asked me to give her some figures. I wrote them down. She must have left the sheet here, on the desk."

"Didn't tear it up, did she? Burn it in the fireplace? All but a couple of scraps? You seem to have explanations for everything, young fellow. Some not so good. Maybe that letter was a demand for money. Maybe you burned it yourself, to cover your tracks. Looks like we'd have to take you down to Headquarters."

Footsteps, along the hallway, drew his attention. A small, neat gentleman, wearing spats and a cutaway coat came into the room, carrying a black leather satchel. Two officers in uniform followed him.

"Hello . . . hello . . . hello!" he murmured, bending over the body. "This is bad."

"It is, Doc," the Inspector agreed. "Very."

"Mrs. Kirby! Well . . . well! Poor woman! I knew her slightly. H . . . m. Peculiar wound. Made by some round, smooth, sharp-pointed instrument."

"Such as a nail?" Duveen inquired softly.

"A nail?" The Medical Examiner glanced up. "Well . . . perhaps . . . a large wire nail. Although I should have expected something a little more tapering. Not quite so

straight up and down if you get what I mean." He turned
the dead woman's head to one side, peering at her throat.
"H . . . m! . . . bruises! She must have been choked, first.
But not to death . . . the face shows too little suffusion.
Then, after she had been rendered unconscious, the nail or
other weapon was used to finish the job . . . couldn't have
been accomplished otherwise. Have you found it?"

The Inspector shook his head; he was not listening.
His eyes were fixed on something which lay on the tan
desk-blotter, hidden, up to now, by Mrs. Kirby's head. A
photograph . . . a snapshot. He picked it up, very carefully, by the edges. The picture showed a stretch of beach.
A Continental beach, to judge from the character of
the buildings in the background. Nearer, two persons, a
man and a woman, stood smiling extravagantly into each
other's eyes, holding each other's hands. The woman, well
past her early youth, wore a brief, very chic bathing suit;
it gave her ageing figure an artificially youthful quality
that was also somewhat pathetic. The man, of powerful
physique, wore trunks, and to Inspector Duveen's eyes was
a stranger. Across the bottom of the photograph, written
in a feminine hand were two names "Nick" and "Bee,"
with between them, like a small, connecting chain, the
words *"Toujours—Toujours—Toujours!"*

The Inspector sighed, irritably. Just when the case
seemed all cleared up, one of those unpleasant obstacles
had arisen which he had visualized while waiting at the
door. Even in that absurd costume . . . it seemed absurd,
now, in the presence of death . . . he recognized the woman in the picture readily enough; a downward glance was
all that was needed to show him her cold, lifeless face.
And while he might be in doubt concerning the man with
her, he *did* know . . . here the Inspector gave a small, harsh
laugh . . . that it was *not* Senator Kirby!

The Medical Examiner straightened his well-tailored shoulders, dusted his slender fingers.

"I can tell you more about the weapon after we've had a post-mortem," he said. "As I have just remarked, the woman was choked to insensibility, probably right where she is sitting now, and while unconscious, a sharp instrument was driven into the base of her brain. Which indicates, I should say, although it is more in your province than mine, that robbery was not the motive."

"Why?" the Inspector asked. "A valuable pearl necklace has been stolen."

"That may be." The doctor's eyes twinkled shrewdly. "But thieves . . . most thieves at least . . . do not commit unnecessary murders. If the man who broke in here . . ."

"It may have been a woman," the Inspector interrupted.

"Indeed! You surprise me. But still not impossible. If the woman who broke in here . . ."

"She didn't break in; Mrs. Kirby apparently admitted her."

"Really? That is even more surprising. But the fact remains that any thief, having once rendered his victim unconscious, could have walked off with the loot in comparative safety. Why stop to commit a perfectly needless murder?"

"If Mrs. Kirby knew who the thief was, she may have been killed to prevent her from telling."

"Possible, but unlikely. Especially such a clean, cold-blooded murder as this. It took coolness, Duveen, to drive that weapon, whatever it was, into her spine with such nice precision. However, that's your job, not mine. I suppose you want to know when death took place. Within the past hour, I should say, well within it. That is all I can tell you, pending a more thorough examination." As he turned to leave, he almost ran into a hurrying figure, suddenly framed in the doorway. A slender, dark man of unusual distinction and charm.

"I . . . Good God! Dr. Ames! What's wrong?" The newcomer's voice broke slightly as he caught sight of the body in the chair.

"Why hello, Dr. Badouine!" The Medical Examiner put out his hand. "Didn't expect to meet you, on a murder case."

"Murder! They . . . they told me Mrs. Kirby had met with an accident. I came at once!"

"Nothing you can do, I'm afraid." Dr. Ames, being of the old school, did not think very highly of psychoanalysts.

Dr. Badouine stood aside as the two uniformed men lifted the body to a couch, covered it with a sheet. His sensitive face showed real grief; he seemed deeply shocked by Mrs. Kirby's death.

"If you had told me suicide," he said.

"Hardly! Strangulation! And a wound at the base of the brain! My dear fellow!" The Medical Examiner chuckled.

"I meant, Dr. Ames, that knowing Mrs. Kirby's mental condition, I should not have been surprised to learn that she had killed herself."

Inspector Duveen pricked up his ears at that.

"Any idea who might have done it, doctor?" he asked. "I'm in charge here. Detective Bureau . . ."

"No." Dr. Badouine shook his head. "No particular person. I may say, however, without violating professional ethics, that Mrs. Kirby has been greatly distressed of late over her daughter's infatuation for a certain foreigner—a titled foreigner—to whom she has become engaged. I am not gossiping; Mrs. Kirby's opposition . . . her very bitter opposition . . . was well known to all her friends."

"H . . . m! Her daughter, eh?" The Inspector saw another disagreeable difficulty appearing. Mrs. Kirby . . . the

Senator . . . and now, the daughter. Pitfalls? Worse! The presence of this photograph under the murdered woman's head was dynamite—no less. Capable of causing all sorts of domestic explosions—even murder. He must step cautiously, now . . . must look beyond a pearl necklace for a solution of the mystery.

"Are there no clues?" Dr. Badouine asked, his voice shaking.

The Inspector plucked a sheet of monogrammed notepaper from the rack upon the desk, folded it about one half of the snapshot. This, while it hid the figure of the woman completely, left that of the man fully exposed to view. Holding the picture between this protective covering, Duveen thrust it under Dr. Badouine's eyes.

"Know who that is?" he asked.

The doctor stared down, nodding.

"Why, yes," he said quickly. "Of course. It's the man I've just spoken of. Miss Jean Kirby's fiancé! Count Nicolas de Zara!"

VI

"So far as murder cases are concerned," Inspector Duveen had frequently been heard to say, "most of them have either too many clues or not enough . . . a feast or a famine. There's no happy medium."

He was thinking just that now, on the heels of Dr. Badouine's identification of the man in the snapshot as Count Nicolas de Zara. Thinking, but not saying anything. There was good reason for silence. So far, no one but himself had seen the photograph, in its entirety, at least. Even the doctor had been shown but half of it . . . the man's half. That the woman in the picture, carefully hidden by a folded sheet of paper, was Mrs. Kirby, the Inspector decided to keep to himself; his thoughts told him that there was nothing medium about *this* case, happy or otherwise. So far as clues were concerned, it had suddenly become overburdened with them.

Until a few moments ago this young fellow Ransom and the girl with him, Miss Vickery, had seemed a pretty safe bet. Strands of dark hair, the color of hers, in the dead woman's fingers. What looked like a demand for money, in the young man's handwriting, upon a scrap of paper found on the floor. A plot to steal Mrs. Kirby's pearl necklace between them, overheard by one of the servants. And now what? A whole series of new and entirely different

possibilities, brought up by the discovery of this photograph!

What was the picture doing under the murdered woman's head? A snapshot, in a risqué bathing suit, linking her
none too pleasantly with a man not her husband. A man,
in fact, engaged to marry her daughter. *"Toujours—Toujours—Toujours!"* The Inspector had learned enough French
with the A.E.F. to understand the tender significance of
that. Had the Senator, discovering the photograph, gone
into a tailspin and decided to do away with a faithless
wife? Or had Mrs. Kirby confronted de Zara with the picture, threatened to show it to her daughter in a last desperate effort to break off the marriage? Coupled, perhaps,
with threats to disinherit the girl as well? Plenty of motive there for murder, to say nothing of the fact that Mrs.
Kirby's death would be greatly to de Zara's advantage,
since Jean, as an only child, would inherit the bulk of her
mother's money! God, what a mess! The Inspector groaned
inwardly.

Other equally unpleasant possibilities suggested themselves. Mrs. Kirby might have shown the snapshot to her
daughter first, hoping in that way to destroy the girl's
infatuation for de Zara. Have arranged a midnight meeting with her, unknown to the servants. The Inspector knew
from the newspapers that Miss Jean Kirby fancied herself a
sculptress, spent much of her time at a studio downtown.
Was she tall, dark? He had seen pictures of her, in rotogra-
vure sections, but did not remember. Could a mother and
daughter be sufficiently jealous of each other to resort to
murder? Or was it not more reasonable to suppose that de
Zara had gone to Mrs. Kirby with the picture, attempted
to use it as a club with which to force her consent to their
marriage? A threat to show it to the Senator might have
brought her to terms or, in case she resisted, to her death.

"Hell!" The Inspector pulled savagely at his moustache. Plenty of clues, all right. Too many. Why, for instance, had the wall safe been exposed? Had Mrs. Kirby opened it, to take the photograph out . . . closed it again? And the documents burned in the fireplace? Where did they fit in the picture? Inspector Duveen suddenly remembered rumors he had heard regarding Senator Kirby's liking for a certain very attractive widow. Could this unknown woman have been Mrs. Kirby's visitor? Perhaps *she* had in some way obtained possession of the snapshot . . . had tried to use it, to get Mrs. Kirby to give her husband a divorce. Was she tall and dark? That was an angle he would have to investigate. And whether Mrs. Kirby . . . God forgive him for thinking ill of the dead . . . having played around with one man, might not also have done the same with another? A man who had somehow got hold of this picture, was trying to blackmail her? Could she have had not one visitor, but *two,* during the evening . . . a woman, and a man . . . ? Then there were this Vickery girl . . . this fellow Ransom . . . The Inspector wiped the sweat from his forehead. Pitfalls, to trap the unwary? Wide gulfs! Morasses! Opening on every hand! Damn such a case! If he didn't watch his step . . .

Inspector Duveen did not lack courage. He had left two fingers and part of an ear in the Argonne and brought back a Congressional medal, but while his trigger finger was still intact it wasn't likely to be of much use in dealing with rich senators, and women—especially women. He did not understand them and was sensible enough to admit it, which, in a man, is the pinnacle of wisdom. He glanced about the room, watched the Medical Examiner go down the hall; no one else had moved since Dr. Badouine's announcement . . . his own mental excursions had taken less than thirty seconds.

Without comment, he wrapped the photograph in another sheet of paper to prevent damage to possible fingerprints, placed it in his pocket. Edward, with Parsons, the second man, hung tentatively just outside the door. Duveen turned to the butler, trying to keep his voice calm.

"Do you know where Senator Kirby is?" he asked.

"I heard him tell Mrs. Kirby, at dinner, he had a political meeting."

"Miss Kirby?"

"I can't say, sir." Edward shook his head. "Miss Kirby has been spending a great deal of time lately at her studio."

Dr. Badouine, staring with somber eyes at the couch, glanced up.

"I think I can tell you about Miss Kirby," he said. "Mrs. Conover, a mutual friend, spoke to her at luncheon today about a bridge game this evening; Jean . . . Miss Kirby . . . couldn't make it, because she was dining with Count de Zara and going on somewhere, afterwards, she said, to dance."

Duveen nodded. Another check; he would have to wait until the girl showed up, if she did. Meanwhile, he might as well question the servant, Parsons. No need to let this young fellow Ransom know that the photograph had turned suspicion in other directions; after all, the picture might not mean as much as he thought.

"You!" he said, pointing a lone forefinger at the man. "Are this lady and gentleman the ones you overheard talking about Mrs. Kirby's pearl necklace?" He nodded over his shoulder.

"Yes, sir." Parsons sidled into the room; he looked like a heavyweight and talked in the piping voice of an adolescent schoolboy. "They planned to murder her; I heard them say so distinctly. And to blame the crime on the butler. 'Take the rap' was the expression the gentleman used."

Steve spoke then. Angrily. He thought the Inspector a fool and wanted to say so.

"Why waste time over that?" he growled. "I've told you it was just a lot of hooey. If I'd been planning to murder anybody you don't suppose I'd have been fool enough to broadcast it, do you? This young lady is tired . . . ought to go to bed! I'm due back in Baltimore! Have we got to stand around here all night?"

"You can sit down if you want to," the Inspector retorted. "Anyway, you won't be going back to Baltimore. I want you both where I can put my hands on you as material witnesses, if nothing else."

"Does that mean you're figuring to lock us up?"

"I may." The Inspector considered. "Not the young lady; she'll be safe, here in the house. But you can't leave Washington."

"Oh, all right! In that case, I'll go to a hotel. I'm not planning to run out on you. If I'd wanted to do that I could have gone long ago; my car's outside."

"With one of my men sitting in it," the Inspector said dryly. "You keep your shirt on, young fellow; I'm bossing this job!"

Dr. Badouine crossed the room, held out his hand. "How do you do, Ransom," he said. "We met at lunch, you remember. Talked about psycho-analysis, in crime detection."

"Of course," Steve nodded. "I remember very well."

"If you find yourself in any difficulties," the doctor went on, "don't hesitate to let me know. Mrs. Kirby was not only a patient, but a friend; I'll be glad to do anything I can to help bring her murderer to justice." A somewhat ironic smile on his intelligent face, he turned to Duveen. "No need to send Mr. Ransom to the lock-up, Inspector; he is a writer of standing. I shall be very glad to vouch for him."

"Thanks, doctor," Steve said. "Mighty decent of you."

"All right, all right!" the Inspector grumbled. "He can go to a hotel if he wants to; we'll see he doesn't run away."

"And look me up tomorrow, Mr. Ransom," Dr. Badouine added, moving toward the door. "We'll have a talk. If I can be of no further service here, Inspector, I'll say good night."

"Nothing to keep you," Duveen said indifferently, his mind on other matters.

Dr. Badouine, with a last shocked look at Mrs. Kirby's body, left the room. One of the Inspector's men came up holding a blackened bit of cardboard between his fingers.

"Found this wedged down behind the backlog, Chief," he said. "Flat against the brickwork; that's why it didn't burn up."

The Inspector's eyes narrowed. Half of a torn correspondence card. In spite of its charred condition a few words were faintly legible. Significant words. "Of value." "Danger." "Talk it over." The signature at the bottom, least burned of all, was "Lawrence Dane."

Duveen sighed. Another clue. Instead of welcoming, he almost resented it. He knew quite well who Lawrence Dane was; the local stock company had an excellent press-agent. How he fitted into this complex picture puzzle was another matter; it was exasperating, the way each new development seemed to upset all the others. He spoke to Edward, sharply.

"Is Mr. Lawrence Dane, the actor, a friend of the family?" he asked.

"Yes, sir. That is, a fairly frequent visitor, sir; I think Mrs. Kirby met him in New York; she knew a good many stage people."

Well, that was that. Another angle to be investigated. He gave one of his men some whispered instructions. Dane, too, might have got hold of the photograph.

A rapid click of heels sounded from the corridor; Duveen turned as a slim, graceful girl swept into the room. For a moment she stood staring about her, wide-eyed, then with a tragic cry ran to the couch, fell on her knees beside it.

"Mother . . . Mother!" she sobbed. "He didn't mean it . . . he didn't mean it!"

Even in that distressing moment the Inspector did not fail to notice that the girl was tall, and wore a long, dark coat. Her hair, however, was ash-blonde. He touched her gently on the shoulder.

"How did you know about your mother?" he asked. The girl looked up, her face wet.

"Dr. Badouine told me! I . . . I just met him at the door!"

The Inspector nodded; he had children of his own, and a mother.

But while his voice was kind, it was also firm.

"Would you mind telling me, Miss Kirby," he asked, "how you spent the evening?" The girl rose, her lips quivering.

"You want to question me?" she demanded. *"Now?"*

"Yes, Miss Kirby. It may help us to find out who murdered your mother."

"Murdered . . . !" Jean Kirby's mobile face became a rigid mask; her eyes, a moment before soft with tears glittered like green jewels. "Dr. Badouine didn't tell me . . . that!"

"Yes, Miss Kirby, I'm sorry to say. Now if you will kindly answer me . . ."

"Very well!" The girl straightened her shoulders, her chin went up. "I dined with Nick . . . Count de Zara . . . my fiancé. Danced afterwards. At eleven I took him back to his apartment, left him there; he had an appointment. After that, as it was early and I didn't feel like going to bed, I drove around."

"Around?" the Inspector queried softly.

"Yes. Nowhere in particular. Out toward Laurel . . ."

"You didn't stop?"

"No."

"Why did you come here? I'm told you've been sleeping at your studio."

"I . . . I came because I'd made up my mind to see . . . Mother." The girl's eyes flicked toward the sheeted figure on the couch. "We'd had a quarrel. A frightful quarrel. About . . . Nick. She didn't want me to marry him. Said I could only do it over her dead body! Nick said that was all right with him . . . that she didn't dare to stop me. He was very angry, lost his temper. Afterwards he felt sorry, said he didn't mean it. I drove around, thinking. Then I decided to come here and tell her so. It seems I arrived too late."

"You say Count de Zara had an appointment. At his studio. Who with?"

"I don't know. He didn't tell me. Some business matter."

The Inspector rubbed the faint stubble of beard along his jaw. De Zara left at his apartment at eleven. The girl just "driving around." Not so good. Tall . . . a long black coat . . . a black toque. The butler, from his third story window, had not seen the woman's face. But the strands of hair in Mrs. Kirby's fingers were not blonde.

"I'd like to have Count de Zara's address," he said.

Jean Kirby snatched a card from her purse, wrote something on it; her fingers were shaking.

"Here! It's the same as mine! I mean I have my studio in the same building! Now go, please. All of you! I want to be alone with . . . with . . ." In spite of her rigid control the girl was close to the breaking point.

"But . . . that's impossible, Miss Kirby." Inspector Duveen tried to be kind. "We have work to do here. And the . . . the body must be sent away for . . . for further examination. Also, I am waiting to see your father. If you happen to know where he is . . ."

The girl's head went up. Some new, not pleasant thought had apparently crossed her mind. She turned toward the door.

"I don't!" she said. "Thank God!" A moment later the patter of her quick running footsteps sounded from the stairway.

The Inspector looked at Edward.

"You were very fond of Mrs. Kirby, weren't you?" he asked.

"Yes, sir, very." The wizened old man seemed close to tears; his chin, covered with a soft grey rime, wobbled uncertainly. "She was very good to me, like a friend, for almost eighteen years."

"Then I suppose you'd like to see her murderer punished?"

"I would indeed, sir. I am a peaceable man, but I think, begging your pardon, sir, I should be glad to place the rope about his neck."

"*His* neck?" The Inspector frowned. "Then you think it was a man?"

"No, sir. Not even after hearing Parsons' story about this gentleman here." The butler glanced fleetingly at Steve. "I used the word 'his' in a manner of speaking, sir. I think Mrs. Kirby was killed by the woman I saw come in."

"Any idea who it was?" Duveen asked swiftly, like a cat, pouncing.

"Yes, sir. As I've told you, I could not see her face, but there was something familiar about her . . . her general outline, if you know what I mean. Her way of walking, sir."

"Ah!" The Inspector felt that he had struck pay dirt at last. "Let's have it!"

"I thought, sir, it might have been Georgette."

"Georgette?" In his surprise and disappointment the Inspector sputtered; he had hoped for a very different answer. Still another suspect, another angle! "Who the hell . . . ?"

"Yes, sir. Mrs. Kirby's maid. The one she brought back, two years ago, from France."

France! Snapshots! Continental beaches! *"Toujours—Toujours—Toujours!"* The Inspector's hands waved in dizzy circles.

"Get her here!" he roared.

"Sorry, sir," Edward's chin was wobbling more than ever, "but she left, a month ago. Or was discharged. I never rightly knew which. Although," he added as an afterthought, "we, meaning the servants, sir, were all very glad to see her go. A snake in the grass, sir, if ever I met one."

"What color was her hair?" the inspector interrupted fiercely.

"Red, sir! Very coarse and red."

"Humph!" Duveen stood silent, thinking. He was thinking of Senator Kirby. Servants, maids, were sometimes bought, used as tools. But the woman's hair was wrong. He asked Edward another question. "Mrs. Kirby, I'm told, had been greatly worried, of late. Upset. What was she worried about?"

The butler stood very still. There was dignity in his pose. His rheumy eyes showed a sudden pale fire.

"It is not my place, sir . . ."

"Skip it! This is murder, man, not a ladies' tea! I know she was worried about her daughter, and this Spig! I just heard that! What else? Anybody been quarrelling with her? Threatening to kill her? Servants always get wise to such things. I'm looking to you for help! Well?"

The butler considered, gravely.

"Perhaps, sir," he muttered, "now that Mrs. Kirby is dead, it is my duty to speak. I make no accusations, sir. But I think the thing that worried Mrs. Kirby most of all . . . even more than her daughter, sir, was the way in which Senator Kirby had been trying to force her to give him a divorce! When she refused, even after he sent his lawyer here, sir . . . they . . . Mrs. Kirby and her husband . . . had a fearful quarrel; you could hear them on the third floor!"

"Is that so?" The Inspector nodded. Husbands rarely insisted on divorces unless there was another woman involved. "Now look here. You told me a while ago Senator Kirby was due at a political meeting. You didn't say it as if you believed it. Well, come again! And come clean, this time! Where is he? I'm not accusing the Senator of any-thing, understand. But I've got to get hold of him quick! So if you know . . . ?"

Inspector Duveen was a bit excited. The footsteps in the hall were curiously soft. Not until a voice interrupted him did he realize that someone was standing in the doorway.

It was a round, sonorous voice, which even in this somber moment seemed unconsciously directed toward a microphone. Rumor said of Senator Kirby that never, even in the midst of heated debate, did he lose his temper. He was keeping it now, although with difficulty.

"You would be wiser, I think," he said frowning, "to address any such questions to me personally." For a mo-ment his gaze passed beyond the Inspector, rested enig-matically upon the sheeted figure on the couch. "Your men have told me what has occurred."

Duveen flushed. He had been doing his duty as he saw it, and the contempt in the Senator's voice angered him. After all, being in Congress didn't make a man God . . . he accepted the challenge, knowing the danger of doing so; he'd expected that, from the start.

"Very well!" he said coldly. "Where *did* you spend the evening, Senator Kirby?"

The Senator's big-framed figure, rude, in spite of his well-cut evening clothes, stirred slightly; he measured the Inspector with scornful eyes.

"Where I spent the evening is my personal and private affair," he said, biting the words off savagely. "And since you have no legal right to ask me such a question, I decline, on the same grounds, to answer it! Your commanding officer, Major Bliss, who happens to be a friend of mine, will be glad I am sure to instruct you regarding the powers of the police in such matters; he would be the last person to countenance such bulldozing methods!"

Inspector Duveen's face turned bright crimson. His fingers . . . the ones he had left, crooked nervously.

"I hadn't any idea of bulldozing anybody, sir," he muttered. "I know you don't have to answer my questions, if you don't want to. I'm trying to clear up the brutal murder of your wife."

"Unless you suspect me of committing it, my whereabouts during the evening have nothing to do with the matter!"

"Only this, sir. By eliminating those who have alibis . . ."

"Nonsense! You're not supposed to pry into my private affairs and I don't propose to let you do it! When, and if, I am accused of anything will be time enough to talk about alibis! You men of the police take entirely too much on yourselves; this is not Russia! Nor do I think under the circumstances," he glanced again at the couch, "that I care to discuss the matter any further just now. Get on with your inquiry, if you are making one; there are plenty of profitable avenues you might pursue. If I can be of any legitimate help in your investigations, you will find me in my study." For a long moment he stood beside the couch staring down at the sheeted figure which lay there, but with what emotions those in the room could not tell, since his back was toward them, his face hidden. Then he stalked heavily down the hall.

"Tough baby!" one of the plainclothes men muttered under his breath. "If he hasn't got something on his conscience, after that blast, I'm the King of Abyssinia and should buy a red parasol!"

The Inspector frowned; his face was purple with anger.

"Pipe down," he said sharply, "and see about getting de Zara and that actor, Dane, out here. I want to talk to them, pronto! Have Carey and Abramson dig them up. You, young woman," he wheeled swiftly on Ann Vickery, "go to bed! It's getting late, and you'll have a lot of explaining to do tomorrow! Hunter," his trigger finger pointed out Steve Ransom, "tell Ryan, he's in this man's car, to take him to a hotel, see he stays there! And make sure, first, he hasn't got any pearls up his sleeve. Before you go, young fellow, write down your Baltimore address."

Steve turned to Ann Vickery, took her hand.

"Good night," he whispered. "This looks like curtains, for the first act. I'll be seeing you tomorrow, about the second. In spite of hell and high water, you know, the play always has to go on. Sorry I got you into it, but that can't be helped now." With a rather rueful grin he went to the Chippendale desk at which Mrs. Kirby's body had been discovered, sat down to write out his address.

There was monogrammed paper in a small rack; he drew out a sheet of it, looked about for a pen. At one side of the desk stood a square malachite base with a metal cup on top of it, from which a slender penholder projected at a rakish angle.

Steve reached forward—checked his fingers in midair. The shining chromium shaft of the holder was slim as a surgeon's lancet. Held in anyone's hand, with the pen-point covered, it could readily be mistaken for a long wire nail!

He turned to the others, curiously watching him.

"I may be wrong, Inspector," he said quietly, "but I rather think here's your weapon!"

VII

The morning was warm, with the softness of spring in it, and Steve Ransom yawned sleepily, thinking that Washington hotels had comfortable beds. His watch showed him it was after nine o'clock.

He read the newspapers over breakfast in his room, while waiting for a bell-hop to bring back a clean shirt and some necessary toilet articles. Mrs. Kirby's murder had made the front page, with banners, but only as part of a jewel robbery; Inspector Duveen was playing his hand close to the chest. The most valuable card in it, the snapshot photograph, still remained an ace in the hole. Once let the news-hawks get wind of that, and there would be a veritable deluge of scandal.

Steve, not having seen the picture himself, understood nothing of the Inspector's responsibility. He knew only that Jean Kirby's fiancé, Count Nicolas de Zara, was a figure in it. Had he visualized a woman in the photograph, she would not by any stretch of his imagination have been the girl's mother. Hence he had thought Duveen's questioning of Senator Kirby rather bullheaded; de Zara, under the circumstances, seemed the most logical suspect.

Lucky, he thought, smiling over his coffee, that the discovery of the picture left Miss Vickery and himself in the clear . . . if it did. Anyway, he hoped so. A damned pretty girl—not pretty, exactly—attractive. Smartly attractive. A thoroughbred . . . clever, with a nice sense of humor. He could go for a girl like that. She hadn't been peevish over the mess he had landed her in, with his loose talk about mystery murders. A lot of women might have been sore.

Of course there was no assurance that they were out of it, yet. So far as he had seen, the Inspector had not made much progress in handling the case . . . hadn't even discovered the weapon until it had been pointed out to him. Steve was rather pleased, over that small success; his vanity was tickled. Why not do a little more work, on his own? That would be better than sitting around the hotel. A writer of detective, of mystery, plays ought to be able to figure out a solution of a real-life drama if he put his mind on it. Helped, perhaps, by that psychiatrist . . . what was his name . . . Badouine. An intelligent egg . . . brains. He had offered any assistance in his power . . . it might be a sound idea to call on him . . . get his ideas, which should be good, as to a possible motive for the crime.

Certainly, Steve reflected, he owed it to this Vickery kid to do anything he could, to get her out of the jam in which he had placed her. With his chatter about stealing Mrs. Kirby's pearls. Not so good. He would drive out to Halfway House, see her, later. Meanwhile, why not do a little work on de Zara? He seemed, after the disclosure regarding the photograph, to be the most likely source of information. The Count would remember meeting him, no doubt, at Mrs. Kirby's luncheon. If he had a telephone . . . Steve consulted the directory, found the number, then decided not to call up . . . it would be better to appear in person, without giving de Zara an opportunity to put him off. There was a chance that, as a more or less disinterested outsider he might be able to secure facts that the Count would not give to the police. Whistling he walked around to the garage where he had left his car.

On the way down Pennsylvania Avenue it occurred to him that it might be an excellent idea to look up the restaurant at which he had eaten supper on leaving the theatre the night before. Inspector Duveen would want confirmation of his alibi.

Steve found the place without much difficulty; a quick-lunch establishment called "Berger's." The proprietor, a dark, shifty little man, had not been on hand the previous evening and seemed to regard inquiries concerning his staff with suspicion. Steve finally managed to drag from him the information that one of his waitresses, Katie Bolek, was home sick. He got her telephone number, but when he called up, a tremulous voice informed him that the girl was seriously ill, with pneumonia, and could see no one.

Steve got back into his car, no longer whistling; fate, it appeared, was working overtime to involve him in Mrs. Kirby's murder. He drove to de Zara's address, more determined than ever to find out, if possible, what motive lay beneath the tragic affair. As the Medical Examiner had said, it could not have been plain robbery.

The number, on G Street was that of a once handsome private residence, now converted into studio apartments. Cards in the vestibule showed that Miss Jean Kirby occupied the top floor. A sculptress would need to be under the roof, of course, for proper light; de Zara, installed on the floor below, evidently did not require special lighting for his particular form of art, whatever it was.

Instead of ringing the vestibule bell, Steve went up the stairs, hammered the antique brass knocker on the studio door.

De Zara himself opened it, after a considerable wait. He wore an embroidered dressing gown over his massive frame, and seemed both sleepy and irritable.

"Well?" he yawned, blinking reddened eyes. "What is it?"

"I'm Stephen Ransom," Steve said. "Met you yesterday, at Mrs. Kirby's luncheon party. Hope I didn't get you out of bed."

"You did," de Zara replied crossly. "I thought it was the police again; they kept me awake until four. That is a terrible business, Mrs. Kirby's murder! The poor woman! Shocking, yes? I cannot understand it. Me, I know nothing. But you must not stand here. Come in, please." He opened the door wide, closed it. "Sit down. We might have a drink, no? I can give you vermouth, Martini Rossi. Or brandy." He snapped up the window shades, brought bottles, glasses, from a carved Jacobean cupboard.

Steve glanced about the long room. Almost the entire floor of the building. There was a day-bed in it, a grand piano, many bits of antique furniture, mostly foreign. The walls, however, were what held his curious attention; almost every inch of them was covered with weapons. Pistols by the hundred, mostly handsome dueling sets, beautifully chased, inlaid. Matchlocks, wheellocks, flintlocks, superb examples of the gunsmiths' art. Fowling pieces, blunderbusses, long Algerian rifles, rapiers and broadswords, German dueling sabers, daggers of European and Oriental make; outside of a museum, Steve had never seen such an elaborate display.

De Zara splashed brandy, neat, into two crystal goblets. "*Santé,*" he muttered, emptying his glass at a gulp, *à la militaire.* "I am fatigued . . . what you say, done, all in, finished! You are looking at my collection? It is nice, eh? That pair of flintlocks you see near the window, the ones with the lacquered stocks, were made in Japan . . . very old. The sport-gun above is from Vienna . . . sixteenth century. Notice the workmanship of the barrels. Exquisite. There are three hundred and twenty pistols, altogether."

"Where did you get them?" Steve asked.

"Oh, here and there. Many, in Paris . . . at the Flea Market. You know the Flea Market, yes? Very interesting. That pair of pikes, near the piano, I picked up one morning for ten francs! They are from the time of François Villon. And the little stiletto there, with the jade hilt . . . from Thibet. But you do not drink your brandy."

Steve raised his glass. He had come to discuss a murder, not weapons for committing one. De Zara, he saw, was highly nervous, rattling on at random, to take his mind from the tragedy.

"What did the police ask you?" Steve said.

"Where I was last night. From eleven o'clock. I told them here. Miss Kirby brought me, after our dancing, to keep an engagement. I did not go out again."

"Then you're all right," Steve said.

"Maybe so, maybe not. The person I was with must also say that. And it is first necessary that I find her."

"Her?" Steve asked, surprised.

"Yes. It was a woman. But not, maybe, as you think. She came, for . . . for another reason, some business."

"I see. And didn't the police question you about the photograph?"

"Photograph?" De Zara's eyes suddenly rounded until they looked like two bright copper pennies. "What photograph do you mean?"

"Why, the one that was found under Mrs. Kirby's head. A snapshot of some sort. You were in it."

"Me?" The Count rose to his feet like some gigantic lay-figure, jerkily, his cheeks livid. "What is this you say? I have heard nothing of any photograph."

Steve, noticing the man's agitation, began to wonder if he had made a break. Well, too late to remedy it, now.

"I didn't see the thing myself," he replied. "Nobody did, except the Inspector. But I know you were in the picture somehow, because . . ."

"*Sangue di Dio!* That is impossible!" De Zara hurled himself toward a small buhl table that stood against the wall. On it was an oblong box, apparently an antique jewel casket, made of dull steel, its surface inlaid with gold, in arabesque patterns. Snatching a key from a silk cord about his neck the Count opened the casket, began to paw frantically through the letters, documents and photographs which it contained.

Presently he turned, his huge shoulders sagging.

"*Maledetto!*" he groaned, waving his hands. "It is gone!"

"What's gone?" Steve asked, although he guessed the answer. If de Zara was not in earnest, he was doing a remarkably fine piece of acting.

"The photograph! The picture of which you speak! There can be but one! On the beach, at Cannes! I took it myself, with a string on the camera shutter. Made but a single copy . . . for remembrance. Even Mrs. Kirby . . . !" He stopped, realizing the slip he had made.

Steve knew, then, who else had been in the snapshot. The knowledge shocked him, set his mind whirling in tragic speculations, as it had that of Inspector Duveen the night before. Motives for murder . . . plenty of them, now . . .

"Somebody must have stolen it!" de Zara mumbled.

"Out of that locked box? How? It's made of steel, isn't it?"

"Yes, yes! Damascus steel. Like the fine sword blades. It could not be cut open, with any ordinary tools. The lock? That might be broken, perhaps . . . but it is not! And the key I wear around my neck!" He stood for a moment, frowning, then crashed his great fist on the table. "That is it! Of course! Now I remember! Not long ago . . . ten days . . . two weeks . . . I have a party. Some friends, to see my collection! In this box I keep, among other souvenirs, a letter from the great Napoleon to one of my ancestors.

From Elba! I take it out, to show to Miss Kirby, to my guests. Then came drinks . . . something to eat . . . I am busy . . . I play the piano . . . *Dio* . . . I forgot the letter . . . do not put it back, lock the box, until the others have gone. Sometime then, that evening, the picture it could have been taken out, stolen! One does not watch one's friends. That screen, at the piano, would shut off the view. You see?"

"Yes," Steve agreed. "Who was here, the night in question?"

De Zara collapsed on a creaking divan, lit a cigarette; his fingers shook so that they could scarcely hold the match.

"Not many. An impromptu affair. Miss Kirby, first, with the nice old man, Judge Tyson, you have met him. And Lawrence Dane, Mrs. Kirby's friend, he is an actor. Then there was Mrs. Conover . . . very charming, that one . . . witty; Dr. Badouine brought her. And Senator Kirby, with his lawyer, small, brown, like a rat; I do not remember his name. Also a woman with them, not young, but very handsome, in the English manner . . . big. It may be she was the brown man's wife; at studio parties one does not inquire. An actress, too, from the stock company, *petite*, with red hair; a friend of Mr. Dane. Counting myself, ten. No more, I think!" Groaning, the Count poured himself another drink of brandy. "But maybe Jean . . . Miss Kirby . . . will remember better."

Steve got up, not entirely convinced. If de Zara wished to disclaim knowledge of the photograph, of its presence at the scene of the murder, he could not have adopted a better plan to shift the responsibility to someone else. Clever . . . and yet, it might also be true. There was a chance that some of the other guests who had been present at the party might know.

"Look here, de Zara," he said. "If anybody stole that picture, as you claim, and we can find out who it was, we'd come pretty close to knowing who killed Mrs. Kirby."

"That is true. It was stolen, as I tell you. If in anyway I can help . . ."

"No." Steve shook his head. "You better keep out of it. And don't let anyone know I told you about that photograph . . . especially the police. I wasn't supposed to tip their hand." He took an envelope from his pocket, wrote down a list of names. "I'll sound out these people. You keep your mouth shut. The less you say about the case right now, the better. By the way, do you happen to know Lawrence Dane's address; I can get it, through the theatre, of course, but it will save time . . ."

De Zara opened the table drawer, took out a leather-covered notebook.

"I think so," he said, riffling the pages. "Yes, here it is, Piedmont Hotel, Eighth Street. You will have no trouble to find the place."

"Thanks." Steve slipped the envelope into his pocket, went over to the wall to examine the small, jade-handled dagger to which de Zara had called his attention. Not far away hung another weapon: a slim, almost needlelike stiletto. Its hilt, of yellowed ivory, spoke of great age, but it was the slender, round blade that first attracted his notice. A lady's poniard . . . something to be concealed in a swirling lace *mantilla* . . . the folds of a bright Spanish shawl. The whole thing was not over nine inches long. But what chiefly interested Steve at the moment was the fact that while the wall behind most of the other weapons showed a uniform coating of dust, the space where the little stiletto hung did not. On the contrary, where its point now lay the faint outlines of a hilt were clearly visible, showing that at some recent date the weapon had been taken from the wall, and replaced in an opposite direction.

De Zara, following Steve's gaze, reached for the little knife.

"You like this one, eh?" he chuckled, holding it in his powerful hand. "The ladies all do. A sharp sting, not so? To carry in the stocking? Many have asked me to give it to them, but I do not encourage such dangerous ideas." Still chuckling, he replaced the dagger on its hook, this time, Steve noticed, as it had originally hung, so that now the pattern of hilt and blade on the wall were properly covered.

Well, that was that. No doubt one of his guests had taken the weapon down and replaced it incorrectly. The Count's action in rehanging it could well have been automatic. His finger prints, of course, would be found on the ivory hilt. All very correct . . . very understandable, but . . .

Somewhat doubtful in mind Steve shook the Count's great paw, left him.

De Zara was yawning like a sleepy, good-natured and rather stupid giant.

VIII

The Piedmont, a small, somewhat run-down, but apparently comfortable family hotel, seemed an ideal place for department clerks, visiting relatives of Congressmen, old gentlemen with nebulous Government claims, and stock-company actors.

Steve gave his name; as he expected, Mr. Dane was not up.

"Tell him," he said to the clerk at the desk, "that Mr. Stephen Ransom, the playwright, wishes to see him." Most actors, he knew, would rise to that bait; they all wanted plays written around them. Mr. Lawrence Dane proved no exception; he would see Mr. Ransom at once. He had just finished shaving when Steve came into the room, and looked freshly pink; his eyes, however, were heavy.

"Hello, hello, old boy!" he exclaimed, extending his hand. "Glad to see you! Delighted!" In spite of his stage training he did not quite succeed in being convincing. "Pardon the looks of this room. And have a highball. There's Scotch on the dresser. White Label. Not bad. I never drink anything else. With a little soda to give it a fizz, it's better than champagne . . . cheaper, too, for a steady diet. Hello!" He picked up the bottle. "A dead one! . . . I must have finished that last night when I got in. This morning, rather; those infernal police kept me up till dawn!"

"You mean about Mrs. Kirby's murder, of course," Steve said.

"Yes. You must have seen it in the papers. Though why the police should think I know anything about the affair gets me. Terrible business! Such a nice woman! Generous! Hospitable!" He opened a closet, set the empty bottle on the floor, took a fresh one from the shelf above. "Mind ringing for some soda while I open this? With ice and a couple of highball glasses? Bit early to start but I need a quick one."

"Not at all." Steve picked up the telephone; over it he saw Dane fish a pocketknife with a corkscrew attached from among a collection of keys, bills and silver coins on the dresser.

Steve watched him open the bottle. The man seemed highly nervous, but whether as a result of too much liquor and too little sleep, or of the grilling he had received at the hands of the police, it was impossible to determine.

"Mrs. Kirby's death was a great shock," Steve said. "You know, I found the body."

"You found the body?" Dane's eyes seemed glazing. "I didn't know! How . . . how did that happen?"

"It's a long story. Anyway, I drove out there last night, walked into the room, found Mrs. Kirby dead. That makes me a suspect, too."

"You don't say?" Dane stood holding the bottle of Scotch in his hands; they were trembling. "Sorry, can't wait for that boy." He tilted three fingers of liquor into a water glass, swallowed it with a shudder. "I needed that! Hair of the dog, you know. How about you?"

"No, thanks," Steve shook his head. "Too early in the day. Besides, I've got work ahead."

"Writing?" Dane seemed glad to switch the conversation to a more congenial subject. "I've always thought that a really fine play could be built around the life of Samuel Pepys. If I had a part like that . . ."

"Not writing," Steve said. "Investigating. That murder. Being a suspect, I can't leave Washington until the matter is cleared up. The police haven't made any progress . . . hadn't, at least, when I left last night. You've seen them since. Was anything said about a photograph?"

"Photograph?" Dane asked.

"Yes. A snapshot of some sort, found under the dead woman's head."

"Well, what about it?" The actor's face remained blank.

"I don't know yet. But I have an idea the picture may have been stolen, perhaps by the murderer, from Count de Zara's apartment during a party he gave there about two weeks ago. You were one of those present . . ."

"Look here!" Dane's fingers tightened on the whiskey bottle, his expression became bleak. "Are you meaning to suggest . . ."

"Oh, no," Steve said easily. "Nothing like that. It may not have been stolen at all. De Zara claims so. In which case, I thought it possible you might have seen one of the other guests snooping around where the picture was kept."

Dane shook his head.

"Sorry, I can't help you there," he said coldly. "The party got going pretty strong, especially after the drinks began to circulate. Almost anyone could have gotten to the box without being noticed."

Steve forced himself to maintain a poker face. How did Dane know where the missing photograph had been kept? 'Gotten to the box!' No mention had been made of any box, until now. Until Dane had himself supplied the word!

"Then you didn't happen to see anybody near it?" Steve went on.

"I did not!" The actor's voice, suddenly harsh, held a note of finality. "When I go to parties I don't watch what people are doing. Might think I was a detective!" He glared at Steve with obvious irritation.

The arrival of the bell-boy with the soda and glasses broke the tension; by the time he had opened it, left the room, Dane was once more smiling and affable.

"I don't quite get the idea, Mr. Ransom," he said, mixing the drinks. "What could this picture you're talking about have to do with Mrs. Kirby's murder?"

"Well," Steve replied, considering, "I haven't seen it myself, of course, but granting the photograph was one of those things that wouldn't look so well, in the newspapers, there's just a possibility it might have been used for blackmail."

"I see," Dane said slowly, his bloodshot eyes narrowing. "Well, that's an idea, at least. You never can tell, about these rich people. Still, it's nothing in my life. Now we can have a regular drink. After that, I'll grab some breakfast and chase around to the theatre. You know what stock is. A dog's life. Different play every week . . . just one rehearsal after another. Let me sweeten that one up for you a little."

He held out the bottle.

"No, thanks. Sorry. And I mustn't keep you . . ."

"That's all right. And I do wish you'd give the idea of a Samuel Pepys play a little consideration. I'm thinking about trying to start a permanent stock company here in Washington. Talented actors, first class productions, put on new plays. You know, like the English actor-managers. There ought to be money in it, handled by the right man. Don't you think so?"

"Possibly," Steve said, his mind on other things. "Guess I'd better be going . . . people to interview . . ."

"Righto! Come again. Always glad to see you. Why not stop around at the theatre some night, after the show, and take supper with me? A play about Pepys, the way you could write it . . ."

"I'll do that," Steve said. "Be seeing you."

On his way to the elevator, he tried to puzzle out what, if anything, Dane knew about the photograph. Of course it was possible that he had mentioned a "box" merely because he saw de Zara take the Napoleon letter from it. After all, such an ornamental casket would be the logical place for a souvenir photograph to be kept. On the other hand, he might very well have made a slip. Have taken the picture, for blackmail purposes, even have murdered Mrs. Kirby. Since he was not on stage during the last act of the play, and thus left the theatre early, there would have been ample time for him to reach Halfway House.

As he turned toward the elevators, Steve glanced up. A slim, cold-eyed young man in a bright tan suit was tapping him on the shoulder.

"Just a minute, buddy," he said. "You're going along with me."

"Guess not!" Steve stepped back, his fists swinging.

"Be good now," the slim man went on, scowling, "before I get tough with you! We're going for a little ride!"

IX

The garden at Halfway House was a pleasant picture under the warm April sun. Ann Vickery looked at the blue lily-pond and thought of Steve Ransom. Even if he had not possessed such amusing eyes, such loose, careless hair . . . just the sort you might like to rumple . . . she would have thought of him anyway, because of the murder.

The clinging horror of it hung over the garden like a grey fog, dimming the spring gaiety of pink dogwood, making the pale snowballs and bridal wreath seem even paler, more ghastly. Mrs. Kirby's body had gone, for the inevitable post-mortem examination . . . Ann shuddered, thinking of that . . . but policemen, reporters, Inspector Duveen and his men still remained to keep alive the grim spirit of tragedy.

Not that Ann needed any such reminder; she had come too close to the core of events, herself. It was only necessary to close her eyes, to see Mrs. Kirby's wax-like face, her dead body bent over the Chippendale desk. In spite of the noisy chirping of birds in the garden she could still hear her high-pitched voice, calling out something about a "nail." Had this meant the shining, lancet-like penholder Steve Ransom had discovered? Ann thought not; there were certain features of that matter she wanted very much to talk over with Mr. Ransom. With Steve. Rather a nice name, Steve, masculine, without being pretentious, like, say, Oliver, or Mark. She had once known a man named Mark; he had insisted on calling her Cleopatra, which was all right, until he tried to make her act the part; she hadn't cared for the name since. Steve, she thought, was more homelike, nothing high-hat about it. She looked up, to see him coming along the box-lined path, the ancient lover's lane. Well, why not?

"Hello!" Steve grasped her hand, squeezed it, almost too enthusiastically for comfort. "How's my little sister in crime this lovely spring morning?"

"Still able to sit up and do her bit," Ann grinned. The shadow over the garden had perceptibly lifted.

"But I thought you said 'moll' was the correct under-world term."

"Say," Steve sank on the bench, "don't remind me of that bunch of tripe. A social error, I'm here to state, considering the trouble it's landed you in. To say nothing of myself. Our friend, the jolly old Inspector, had me collared this morning. By one of the plainclothes johnnies he's had tailing me around.

I thought the bird was a gunman, at first, all set to take me for a ride."

"Really?" Ann said. "What did he want?"

"I don't know. Haven't seen Duveen yet; he's enjoying a session with the press boys, I understand. Or else upstairs. Anyway, he wasn't in the morning room when I arrived so I came out here, hoping to find you. My lucky day, apparently. How's everything going? Any new dope on the crime?"

"If there is," Ann smiled, "Inspector Duveen hasn't confided it to me. I've only seen him once, just for a moment; his manner wasn't friendly. Rather on the Simon Legree side, if you get what I mean. However, I guess it's natural;

the poor man hasn't had any sleep. I heard Senator Kirby storming at him, long after I went up to bed."

"He would," Steve grumbled. "I don't like that old buzzard; he had a guilty look in his eye, last night."

"And later on, so Edward tells me," Ann resumed, "they brought Lawrence Dane, the actor, out here, and Count de Zara. It must be frightful, for Miss Kirby. Losing her mother, and having her fiancé mixed up in an affair like this as well."

"Seen her this morning?" Steve asked.

"Just for a moment. She's lying down; I don't imagine the poor girl slept any. Dr. Badouine is with her now. And Judge Tyson was here; you met him yesterday, didn't you? He is . . . was . . . Mrs. Kirby's attorney, Edward says; he and the Inspector opened the wall safe in the morning room right after breakfast."

"Hear what they found in it?"

"Not officially. But Parsons, the sweet young thing who listened in on our play scenario, told Edward they'd taken out a small fortune in unregistered bonds, and he heard the Judge say Mrs. Kirby never kept anything of value in there, ordinarily, and that she'd been down to her safe deposit box yesterday morning, and must have gotten the bonds out then. I don't know how true this is, possibly just servants' gossip; Parsons strikes me as being one of the ear-to-the-keyhole kind you can't believe. But if there were any bonds in the safe, and the murderer knew it, that probably accounts for the Della Robbia plaque being swung open."

"Queer!" Steve muttered. "Darned queer. The way this case refuses to hang together. Take those bonds. If Mrs. Kirby got them out of her safe deposit box, brought them here to the house, it must have been because she'd arranged to pay them over to somebody. To de Zara, say, as a bribe for not marrying her daughter. Or to that mysterious woman caller, who might have been mixed up in some way with her husband. With the Senator. Or to Lawrence Dane; I have a notion he's concerned in this, somehow. But here's the hitch. If she brought the bonds to pay over to somebody, why didn't she do it? Why was she murdered before she could open the wall-safe? It doesn't work out. Any more than that crazy thing you heard her say about a 'nail.' Of course she may have meant the penholder, but I don't see . . ."

"No." Ann shook her head. "It couldn't have been the penholder. I wanted to talk to you about that."

"Why couldn't it? An ideal weapon . . ."

"Oh, I don't mean it wasn't the weapon, I mean it wasn't what she cried out about. In the first place, if anyone tried to murder me with a thing like that, I wouldn't be apt to waste time, making comments on the nature of the weapon, would I? Hardly. I'd be yelling for help. And in the second place, the Medical Examiner distinctly said last night that Mrs. Kirby wasn't murdered until she had first been choked, made unconscious. Couldn't have been; she wouldn't have held still long enough. In which case she probably never saw the weapon. Isn't that sense?"

"Sense!" Steve exclaimed. "My dear girl, it's positive genius! The next time I write a detective play, I want you as a collaborator."

"I thought 'inspiration' was the correct literary term," Ann said, grinning. "I knew a poet once . . . but that's another story. Anyway, whatever it was that made Mrs. Kirby cry out, it couldn't have been the weapon. You'd better put a little thought on that."

"I have. A lot. So far, no soap. Except . . . wait a minute . . . how about the plaque that hid the wall-safe? The secret spring you'd have to press, to open it. Might be the head of a nail, an ornamental nail . . ."

"We can look," Ann said. "What have you been doing this morning, to help the good cause along?"

"Well, for one thing, I've seen de Zara. He says that photograph . . . it was a snapshot taken on the beach at Cannes, by the way, of himself and Mrs. Kirby . . ."

"Of himself and Mrs. Kirby!" Ann gasped. "And found under the murdered woman's head! Why then, he must have been there, must have killed her!"

"I don't know. He swears somebody stole the picture from his studio. That's a pretty fair out, if he can make it stick."

"Now I understand," Ann said, "why Jean Kirby looked so frightened when I saw her this morning. Not just grief over her mother's death. Something else. Scared stiff, I suppose, about de Zara."

"But why? He claims to have a perfectly good alibi. An engagement at his studio. Of course Jean won't be very happy when she finds out whom his engagement was with; de Zara told me it was a woman . . ."

"No," Ann said. "She won't. But not just the way you mean. Inspector Duveen had the lady in question out here this morning, Edward tells me. Who do you think she was? Mrs. Kirby's French maid!"

"What?" Steve almost fell off the backless stone bench. "Then Edward may have been right in saying he recognized her as Mrs. Kirby's midnight caller."

"Possibly. But it seems the woman swears she didn't leave de Zara's place until after twelve o'clock! And so, of course, does the Count. But don't forget that Edward told us last night Georgette is a fiery henna blonde, and those hairs in Mrs. Kirby's fingers didn't come from any red-head, real, or out of a bottle."

"Which leaves us," Steve groaned, "exactly where we were before, if not more so. My head is beginning to ache . . . and not from being swelled, either. Right now it would

fit perfectly on a plain, ordinary common or garden pin."
He glanced up, saw Dr. Badouine coming across the lawn.
"There's the man I want to talk to. The secret of this case
lies in the motive. That should be right up a psycho-analyst's alley. And he offered, last night, to help."

The doctor, a cheerful figure in heather-grey tweed,
came up to them, smiling. Steve rather admired medical
men who did not insist on dressing like professional pall-
bearers. Dr. Badouine held out his hand; despite the strain
of the previous evening, there were no lines of fatigue in
his clever, intellectual face.

"I heard you were here, Mr. Ransom," he said. "Has
Inspector Duveen got over the rather fantastic idea that
you had anything to do with Mrs. Kirby's death? You might
point out to him that desperate murderers do not usually
telephone the police, and then wait around until they
arrive in order to be arrested."

"Thanks. I shall, when I see him. Haven't, so far. Meanwhile I've been trying to do a little sleuthing on my own."

"Any success?"

"Not much. I'm beginning to think that as a detective
I'm a pretty good playwright. I *did* strike a sort of trail,
though, talking to Count de Zara. It led to an actor, Lawrence Dane. But just what it means . . ."

"Dane?" Dr. Badouine said. "How could he come into
the matter?"

"Don't know, yet. That's what I've got to find out. There
may be a motive no one has hit on, so far. Some curious
mental twist. I thought, such things being right in your
line, maybe you'd be willing to talk it over. How are you
fixed for time? I don't mean now; Inspector Duveen has
me on the carpet. But later, perhaps we could discuss it."

Dr. Badouine glanced at his watch.

"I shall be free at two o'clock," he said gravely. "As it
happens, Mrs. Kirby was to come to me then. If the hour

has not been filled, and I feel sure my secretary would have informed me, I shall be glad to see you."

"Fine!" Steve said. "I'll be there, unless Duveen takes a notion to put me in the hoosegow, meanwhile. Miss Vickery and I are still on his list of suspects, and as it's largely my fault, I'd like to do anything I can."

"Of course, of course." The doctor smiled. "I confess that I myself, as I mentioned when talking to you yesterday, have a sneaking ambition to shine as a sort of mental Monsieur Dupin. Most of us feel that way, I suspect. It's the instinct of the chase. Good day. I must get back to the office." He bowed, went quickly up the path.

"Nice guy!" Steve said. "Brains. I wonder what this buxom lad is after?" A stout policeman was approaching the bench.

"Inspector Duveen wants to see you," he said.

"Meaning me," Steve asked, "or the lady?"

"Both."

"Right!" Steve got up. "I want to see him. Come along, inspiration. I'll probably need you."

Just inside the east wing they met Judge Tyson, talking in low tones to Senator Kirby's small, sandy-haired lawyer, Luke Reed. The latter glanced up sharply as the door opened and with a final, whispered word scurried off along the corridor.

"Terrible affair . . . terrible!" the Judge muttered, grasping Steve's hand. "Who would have thought, when we were talking about murders here yesterday, that within a few hours history would repeat itself?"

"You surprise me," Steve said. "If I remember correctly, the murder you told us about then—the one which took place when this house was an inn—concerned a jealous husband, killing his wife."

"Good Heavens!" Judge Tyson's face, which Steve had thought so genial the day before, was suddenly hard as granite. "Certainly I meant to suggest no such dreadful comparison. You should be more careful, young man, in drawing conclusions, especially at a time like this! Senator Kirby . . ."

"No harm meant." Steve laughed. "Speaking entirely in the abstract. Any new developments?"

"None," the Judge replied, fiddling with his nose glasses, "that I feel at liberty to discuss. Now if you will pardon me . . ." He hurried down the corridor after Luke Reed.

"Now what do you suppose that adds up to?" Steve whispered, turning to Ann. "I apparently got the old boy's goat. Everybody in this affair seems to have something on his or her conscience, darling, except us and I'm not entirely sure we haven't, the way things are going now."

"Well," Ann whispered back, "as the author of the piece, according to Parsons, at least, I fully expect you to provide a few novel and dramatic situations. How do I know, for instance, that you didn't murder the unfortunate lady yourself? Before I came downstairs?"

"You don't," Steve grinned, "any more than I know you didn't do the same thing, before I came into the house. It's fifty-fifty. Anyway, the second act has only just begun; you can't tell what I may have up my sleeve for a climax."

They met Inspector Duveen coming down the stairs beyond the morning room door.

"Couple of questions," he said, waving them inside. "Did you find me the name of that lunchroom, young fellow; I want to check your alibi."

"Yes," Steve said. "It's Berger's. The alibi's shot because the girl who waited on me—her name's Katie Bolek—is in bed with pneumonia. Can't see anyone."

"H . . . m." The Inspector sat down at the Chippendale desk, made some notes on a sheet of paper. "That's just too bad."

"Why?" Steve frowned. "I didn't suppose I was really under suspicion."

"Everybody's under suspicion," Duveen replied coldly, "until they're in the clear. What's the big idea, your going to see Count de Zara? And Lawrence Dane?"

"Why not? Trying to help myself, of course. And Miss Vickery. By finding out, if I can, who's guilty."

"Little amateur detective work, eh? Well, you better stop it. First thing you know, you'll have the case all messed up. What did de Zara tell you?"

"For one thing," Steve said, "he told me about his alibi, his engagement with a woman. Mrs. Kirby's ex-maid, I hear. He didn't say what he was seeing her about. But if she's a red-head, that strengthens his story, because those black hairs Mrs. Kirby had in her fingers would let the woman out."

The Inspector stared down at the desk-top, frowning; he seemed tired, worn. Suddenly he raised his eyes.

"Those black hairs, young fellow," he snapped, "don't let anybody out! They're phony! Dead hairs! Came out of a wig!"

"You . . . you mean," Steve stammered, "that . . . that the woman was disguised?"

"Sure. What else? The woman . . . or man."

"Man?" Steve's head went up. "Then . . . then it could have been Dane?"

"Dane?"

"Of course. He's medium height . . . about right for a tall woman. Smooth-faced. Knows all about disguises, make-up."

Duveen was thinking of the torn, half-burned correspondence card, with Dane's name on it, which had been found in the fireplace. He had already reached certain conclusions regarding the actor but saw no reason for telling Steve Ransom about them.

"Might be," he said. "Anything else against him?"

"Yes," Steve said. "I'm sure he knows something about that photograph."

"Photograph?" The Inspector growled, his eyes hardening. He had supposed the secrets of that picture were known only to himself.

"Sure! The one you found under Mrs. Kirby's head. And showed to the doctor, Dr. Badouine, last night. He said the man was de Zara . . ."

"What does Lawrence Dane know about that picture?" Duveen's voice was not gentle.

"Why . . . I can't tell you, exactly," Steve went on. "De Zara said somebody had stolen it from his apartment, during a party he gave not long ago. Said Dane was there . . . one of the guests. So I asked Dane about it, and while he swore he knew nothing of any photograph, I think he was lying, because he accidentally mentioned the box de Zara kept it in, and I hadn't said anything about a box."

The Inspector stood up. His face was pink with anger. Only too well he knew what would happen if knowledge of that damning snapshot reached the newspapers.

"You keep out of this case," he stormed, "or I'll lock you up where you'll have to! And I don't want you speaking of that photograph to anyone . . . not anyone, get me! I suppose you know who else was in it?"

"Yes, de Zara told me."

"You spill that to Dane?"

"No. I haven't mentioned the matter to anybody, except Miss Vickery."

The Inspector sighed; he had little faith in women, when it came to keeping secrets.

"Then don't. Or you either, Miss. I mean about Mrs. Kirby being the other figure. That's an order. You can see what would happen, if the story ever got around!"

"Yes," Steve said. "I can. It won't through me, Inspector. Or Miss Vickery either. I can promise you."

"I give you my word of honor," Ann added. She rather like Inspector Duveen, even if he did make her think of Simon Legree.

He was looking now at a red-bearded man in khaki overalls who had come to the door opening from the solarium, along with a somewhat younger companion. They bent over the vase of hydrangeas.

"Get a good hold, now, Joe," the bearded man said. "There's some heft to her."

"What's the idea, boys?" the Inspector inquired, watching them suspiciously.

The older man looked up.

"Taking this plant back to the conservatory," he replied.

"Why?"

"Well!" The bearded man scratched his head. "For one thing, because this lady," he glanced at Ann Vickery, "told us to."

The Inspector swung around, his suspicion blazing. "How come?" he asked harshly.

"Why," Ann said, a bit confused by his manner, "I suggested to Mrs. Kirby, yesterday, that the hydrangeas would make a nice spot of color, for her luncheon party. You see, I . . . I'm an interior decorator. But of course hydrangeas don't bloom, in the open air, in April. They have to be forced. Raised under glass. That's why I spoke to the head gardener . . . told him he had better see that the plant was taken back."

The Inspector nodded.

"I thought there was something funny about those big blue flowers," he said, going over to the marble vase. "Sort of stuck in my craw they weren't just right for this time of year." For a moment he stood gazing down at the cluster of blossoms, then his hand shot out, its gaunt trigger finger pointing.

"Lift up that tub!" he exclaimed.

"Tub?" The head gardener rubbed his short carrot-red beard, staring.

"I said tub, didn't I?" the Inspector repeated. "Lift it out, and be quick about it!"

The hydrangea plant was growing in a circular wooden pot, painted green, and equipped with black iron handles. It set loosely inside the somewhat larger bowl of the marble vase.

"My orders were," Duveen went on, "that nothing was to be removed from this room until it had first been searched. Get me?"

"Yes, sir."

The two men, taking the tub by its. handles, lifted it clear of the vase, set it down on the tiled floor of the solarium.

Inspector Duveen paid no attention to them; he was peering at the curved bottom of the marble bowl. Suddenly he reached down, his left hand making a swift, circular movement, in the manner of a scoop.

When he raised it, opened his fingers, a dozen or more round, pink globules lay in his palm.

With a harsh, unpleasant chuckle he extended them toward Ann Vickery.

"Reckon," he said, "they must be Mrs. Kirby's pearls!"

X

Steve Ransom looked from the pearl in Inspector Duveen's hand to Ann Vickery's face and saw there the same confusion he felt himself, at this astonishing discovery. The girl's surprise, her sudden fear, might have been reflected from his own features.

He tried desperately to keep his feelings under control. To doubt her now, to show even a suggestion of doubt, would be fatal, so far as their future relations were concerned. Actually, he felt none; his fear was based on the doubts that others might entertain. Inspector Duveen, for instance; was making no effort to hide his suspicions, although he did not voice them until he had sent the gardener and his assistant from the room.

"You gave orders, miss, did you," he asked, "to have these flowers, this vase, taken back to the conservatory?"

"Yes," Ann said. "This morning."

"Why?"

"The plant might be killed if left here."

"Strange, your being so worried over a hydrangea bush, after all that happened last night! Wouldn't have thought you'd have remembered it, under the circumstances."

"I'm fond of flowers." Ann's voice shook a little but her eyes met the Inspector's steadily.

"Fond enough, maybe," he went on, "to go out to the conservatory, after the plant was carried back there, and collect a small fortune in pearls! Gather 'em up at your leisure, while you're supposed to be admiring the pansies or something!" The Inspector glowered at the small, shining objects in his hand. "Pretty neat, I'll say."

"Rot!" Steve growled. "How could she have lifted that heavy tub?"

"Anything to prevent you from helping her, young fellow?" The Inspector bent down, collected the remainder of the pearls from the bottom of the vase, dropped them carefully into his pocket. "Kind of funny," he went on, "the way you two keep bobbing up in this case."

"Nuts!" Steve exclaimed. "Just because . . ."

"I know . . . I know." Inspector Duveen waved his hand wearily. "But it's a fact, all the same. You just happen by, last night, to look at the moonlight or something. Miss Vickery gives us a lot of hatter about 'nails,' and clocks striking wrong. But the fact remains that you were both right here, on the job, and you did discuss plans for stealing Mrs. Kirby's jewelry, her pearls, beforehand! Now I find 'em in a vase the young lady seems in a mighty big hurry to get off the premises!"

"Are you by any chance accusing us of Mrs. Kirby's murder?" Steve asked, trying to control his temper.

"I'm not accusing anybody . . . yet. But it's just too bad you can't produce an alibi."

"I've explained about the waitress."

"Sure. You're good at explaining. Say the girl *is* sick . . . how do I know you didn't send her home, soon as she brought your order, to get rid of her? Leave you free to come out here fifteen minutes earlier than you say you did, and nobody to tell us you just ate and ran. Like that story about you and Miss Vickery discussing the plot of a play, when Parsons heard you. How do I know that isn't just a cover-up, too?"

"Like my finding the pen for you, I suppose!" Steve retorted. "Thanks."

"Well, why not? I thought it funny, your knowing so much about the weapon . . . if it was the weapon. Not a bad stall, either, considering that penholder had been carefully wiped off."

"Good Lord, man!" Steve's eyes were furious. "Do you think I could kill a woman . . . that way?"

"I don't know. You could have choked her. Maybe Miss Vickery was the one who finished the job, knowing if she didn't, Mrs. Kirby, when she came to, would accuse her . . ."

"That's a lie!"

"Maybe. But I hear from New York the young lady once studied to be a trained nurse, and might know just how to drive a sharp-pointed instrument into the proper spot in somebody's spine."

"Oh!" Ann turned a flat white; she seemed choking.

"Shut up, damn you!" Steve roared. "You know well enough she didn't do it! You know Mrs. Kirby was murdered on account of that photograph!"

The Inspector shook his head; he was very patient.

"That's just what I don't know," he replied. "Seems to me if anybody connected with the picture killed her, they'd have been a fool to go away and leave evidence like that lying around. Pointing right at them. Maybe the photograph was brought, left here by that woman who called, and after she'd gone you folks got busy, on account of the pearls. You said yourself you saw somebody leave through the garden. Maybe the photograph and Mrs. Kirby's death are two separate jobs. Maybe they haven't anything to do with each other. At least that's how it looks to me now. You can't get away from the fact that if this unknown caller committed the murder, she, or he, would never have walked off and left a quarter of a million dollar necklace behind. Whoever hid those pearls in the vase, it must have been somebody who knew they'd be able to get at them, later on. Somebody in the house. And unless you are ready to accuse Mrs. Kirby's daughter . . ."

"Nonsense!" Steve snarled. "She isn't the kind of girl who'd murder her mother. Or steal her jewelry either! Especially as she'd get it all anyway, in the long run."

"That's just how I figure it, young fellow." The Inspector gave Steve a frosty smile. "That's what makes things look so bad right now for you two. Unless Miss Kirby was working with her boy-friend, de Zara . . . I can't see . . ."

The Inspector paused as the door behind him was pushed open. Jean Kirby came into the room. Her tall, fine figure drooped a little under the weight of her grief; her cheeks were like dry clay; against them the dark circles of her eyes seemed enormous.

"I heard what you just said, Inspector Duveen," she whispered huskily. "I couldn't talk last night, I was too upset, frightened. I still am. But I've been thinking things over. Aren't you satisfied with Nick's . . . with Count de Zara's alibi? I understand Georgette has confirmed it."

"Well," Duveen admitted, "their story isn't conclusive. If he and the maid were working together, they'd naturally back each other up. Nothing to prevent that French girl from coming out here, seeing your mother, murdering her, maybe, and then going back to the apartment, swearing she and the Count were together all the time."

Jean Kirby raised her chin.

"Very well," she said. "If that's what you think I may as well tell you the whole story. I would have, last night, if I hadn't been so frightened, so . . . shocked, by what had occurred. I didn't drop Count de Zara at his apartment at eleven o'clock and drive around alone. That wasn't true.

I don't lie, as a rule. It's rather cheap, I think. But last night I was confused . . . afraid. So I said the first thing that came into my head. I didn't leave Nick at his studio. I stayed there with him. And Georgette. Until after twelve o'clock."

"Why?" the Inspector asked coldly, doubt in his still, blue eyes.

"I was afraid you'd ask that. It's one reason I hesitated to speak last night. I knew you'd want to know why Georgette Masson was there. Now I will tell you, since I must. Two years ago my mother had an affair with Count de Zara, at Cannes. That was before he came to America, met me. A harmless enough flirtation, I believe, although it's unimportant now. Just a middle-aged woman, neglected by her husband, flattered by the attentions of a polished, younger man. Nick told me all about it, weeks ago . . . when he proposed. This girl, Georgette, was with mother, at Cannes, knew about the affair. Later, when the Count came to America, began to pay attention to me, Georgette went to mother, blackmailed her. Not for much . . . just petty graft. Naturally you can see how mother would have resented the story getting around. Even an innocent story would have made her the laughingstock of her friends. So she paid Georgette to keep her mouth shut. A month ago, the woman left. I didn't know why, then. I do, now. She was after bigger game."

"You mean the Count?"

Inspector Duveen asked.

"Yes. As soon as she found out Nick wanted to marry me, she began to bother him. She knew, you see, that mother was opposed to our marriage . . . overheard us quarrelling about it, I'm afraid. So she went to Nick and threatened to tell me about the affair, unless he agreed to pay her a lot of money. Nick laughed at her, said I knew about it already. Georgette didn't believe him . . . thought he was bluffing. So he arranged with me to meet the woman at his studio last night to prove to her I didn't care a rap what she said. That I was going to marry Nick in spite of it . . . in spite of anybody."

"H . . . m." The Inspector said. "You mean, then, Miss Kirby, that you're prepared to back up Count de Zara's alibi by swearing on oath you were with him at his apartment last night? At the time your mother was . . . killed."

"Yes!" Jean Kirby replied steadily. "I am."

"Then if that's the truth, and you're not merely trying to shield a man you're in love with, why didn't de Zara tell me so when I questioned him last night?"

"I imagine, being a gentleman, he didn't want to involve me in a scandal. He would have had to explain why I was there, you see."

"And why didn't the maid, this Georgette, say so," the Inspector went on relentlessly, "when I questioned her this morning?"

For the first time Jean Kirby hesitated; she seemed not quite sure of herself.

"I don't know. Unless she was afraid to. Count de Zara told her last night if she ever breathed a word of scandal about either me or my mother he'd . . . break her neck!"

"He wouldn't be likely to break it, Miss Kirby," the Inspector interrupted coldly, "for saying something that may save his own. Don't you realize that unless this Masson woman confirms the statement you have just made, it isn't worth anything? So far she hasn't, and I don't mind telling you I'm keeping her locked up where nobody is going to tip her off."

"She's afraid of him, I tell you! Of Count de Zara!"

"Afraid he'd commit murder? Do you think he would?"

"Yes. So would you, if anybody attacked the good name of your sweetheart, your mother!"

The Inspector looked at Steve.

"If all this is true, young fellow," he said, "it makes things that much worse for you and Miss Vickery."

"Miss Vickery?" Jean Kirby went up to the girl, put an arm about her. "That's absurd. Why should she, or Mr. Ransom, wish any harm to my mother?"

"They could have been after her pearls."

"Her pearls? You mean her pearl necklace?"

"Of course. Somebody got it!"

Jean stared at the Inspector, surprised.

"I don't understand you," she said. "Of course I know very little about the case, except what I heard during the few moments I was in this room last night. I've been trying to sleep, ever since. But my mother's pearls were not stolen."

"How do you know?" The Inspector exclaimed.

"I know, because I have them!"

"*You* have them?" Inspector Duveen's eyes, until now a little bored, flashed with new suspicion. "How is that?"

"It's quite simple. Mother wore the necklace at her luncheon yesterday. When it was over, she called me to her room, gave me the string, told me to keep it for her until morning. I don't know why . . . didn't ask her. She'd done the same thing once or twice before. Mother was always careless about her jewelry. I've been wondering since then, if she'd arranged to meet somebody alone here last night, whether she could have thought it wiser not to have the necklace on her person."

"I see," the Inspector said coldly.

"So she gave it to you?"

"Yes. Just to keep for her overnight, I mean . . . not permanently."

"I see," the Inspector repeated, even more coldly. "And what did you do with the string?"

"Why . . . I put it in my purse."

"You did, eh? Put a valuable thing like that in your purse, and went out to dinner?"

"Yes. With Count de Zara."

"And according to your story, you were with him all evening, until you came back here, at one o'clock?"

"Of course. What are you hinting at?"

"Just trying to get the facts. At one o'clock, you came into this room, stayed five or six minutes, then went up to your suite on the floor above. Right?"

"Certainly it's right. And I still don't see the point of your questions."

The Inspector frowned, his eyes hardening.

"The point is this, Miss Kirby," he said. "If you carried those pearls around with you in your purse all evening, you must have them now."

"But I told you I had them," Jean Kirby said, a gleam of bewilderment in her eyes.

"Where?" Duveen snapped the question like the lash of a whip, at the same time watching the girl's eyes to see if they would turn toward the clump of hydrangea blossoms, the marble vase at the solarium door. Instead, to his disappointment, they dropped to the *suede* bag she held clutched in her fingers.

"Why, here!" she exclaimed, opening it.

Duveen watched the girl narrowly, a trace of amusement in his frosty blue eyes. He was waiting for her to cry out, to assert that someone had stolen the necklace from her during the night.

Instead, she raised her hand, held before his astonished eyes a superb string of perfectly matched pink pearls!

XI

Inspector Duveen was not often taken by surprise; in such cases he usually managed to conceal his feelings behind a suitable mask.

On this occasion, however, his *savoir faire* failed him; he was left blinking. One of his hands, the left one, because of its full complement of fingers, slid into his coat pocket, came out again, in a gesture almost automatic.

"What do you know about these?" he asked.

Jean Kirby bent to examine the half-dozen small, iridescent globes that rolled in the palm of his hand.

"Imitations," she said. "Not very good. Mother bought a string like that in Paris for eight hundred francs. She used to laugh, when her friends couldn't tell them from her real ones. It's not easy, at a glance. But as soon as you compare them," she draped the genuine necklace over Inspector Duveen's outstretched fingers, "you see?" The delicate sheen and luster of the real pearls was unmistakable.

The Inspector saw nothing . . . but red. Someone, he felt, had tried to make a monkey of him, by planting false clues. His mental vision took on an even more magenta shade when he glanced at the message one of his men handed from the doorway.

"Hoffman," it read, "just telephoned that the pearl turned over to him in the Kirby case is phony."

Inspector Duveen crumpled the note between his fingers. The look he gave Jean Kirby was unfriendly. He was thinking that if de Zara, or the maid, had murdered Mrs. Kirby, stolen her necklace, the story he had just heard was excellently designed to protect them. Not that he was prepared to accuse the girl of complicity in her mother's death, but she might be willing, after the event, to try to keep her sweetheart out of it! How simple, how easy, to say the real string had been given her by her mother; the statement could never be disproved, now. And how equally simple, to drop the imitation pearls into the flower vase, thus making it appear that these were the ones Mrs. Kirby had been wearing at the time of her death! As for the suddenly offered alibi, it sounded as artificial as the pearls themselves.

"Miss Kirby," he said, "I think I had better keep this necklace for the present. Until after the inquest, at any rate. If your story, that you were with Count de Zara from eleven until twelve last night, is true . . ."

"Then you doubt it?" Jean Kirby exclaimed, indignant.

"I must until your statement is verified."

"In which case you will be making the very mistake the murderer hoped you would make," the girl went on angrily. "When he left that photograph behind. Or she . . . in case it was a woman!"

"Photograph?" The Inspector's eyes narrowed to hot blue slits. "What do you know about any photograph?"

"I know one was found, because Edward told me so. And I know, if Nick . . . if Count de Zara was in it, that it could only have been left to incriminate him."

"Then you've seen the picture, have you?"

"Of course. Nick showed it to me when . . . when he told me about what happened at Cannes . . . proposed. I've explained all that to you."

"But you haven't explained, Miss Kirby," the Inspector's voice dripped acid, "how, if the picture was in Count de Zara's possession, anybody else could have brought it here, left it on your mother's desk, last night!"

"Oh!" The girl drew back, her shoulders sagging. "You mustn't think . . . you couldn't, that Nick would have . . ."

"I've already told you, Inspector," Steve began hotly, "what de Zara said . ."

He got no further. Duveen turned on him with a black scowl.

"Never mind what de Zara said!" he shouted. "I'm asking this lady now!"

"And I can't tell you," Jean whispered. "I . . . I don't know!" The girl was sobbing pitifully, as though about to collapse. Ann Vickery went up to her and took her arm.

"You'd better rest awhile, Miss Kirby," she said, eyeing Duveen angrily. "I'm sure you are in no shape to be questioned further."

"All right." The Inspector nodded, watching the two women through the door.

Steve lit a cigarette, sat on the arm of a chair.

"I didn't mean to butt in, Inspector," he said, "but I feel kind of sorry for that girl."

"So do I." Duveen stood staring at the hydrangea vase. "Murder cases aren't joy-rides. Take my advice, young fellow, and keep your nose out of this one. I've been pretty easy with you, so far, but don't take advantage of it. Understand?"

"I do. And believe it or not, I'm trying to help. By the way, as long as I made the suggestion I did about that penholder last night, would you mind telling me what the post-mortem showed? Was it really the weapon? I have a reason for asking."

"Looks so. It fitted the wound. But a lot of other things might have fitted it, too. That puncture in Mrs. Kirby's neck wasn't very deep. Didn't have to be, to reach the spinal cord. Just an inch or so. Plenty of things might have been used. Even an ice-pick. Why?"

"Just an idea," Steve said, thinking of de Zara's small stiletto. "I'll let you know, if anything worth while comes of it. By the way, I seem to remember a couple of dogs, about the house. Saw them yesterday. Scotch deerhounds. You'd think they'd have made some sort of a row."

The Inspector nodded wearily.

"Any more bright ideas?" he growled. "Next thing you know, Colonel Bliss will be hiring you as a brain trust. Those dogs were locked down cellar. In the west wing. Always are, at night." He chewed for a moment on his cigar. "Look here. About those phony pearls. I don't want that story to get to the newspapers."

"It won't, from me," Steve laughed. "Now, if you have no objections, Inspector, I'd like to go and see Dr. Badouine."

"What do you want to see him for?"

"I'm hoping to get his help," Steve said quietly. "He's an intelligent guy, for one thing. And for another, he knows all the persons concerned. I may be all wrong, but it seems to me a little psychiatry . . ."

"Huh!" The Inspector gave a short and very expressive grunt.

"The doctor said he'd be free at two o'clock," Steve went on, "in case I cared to come. So if you don't mind . . ."

Inspector Duveen regarded Steve steadily for a long moment, his opaque, china-blue eyes singularly expressionless.

"All right," he said at length. "Go ahead. If he gives you any good leads, come back here and tell me about them. Hunter!" He called down the hall. "Let Mr. Ransom have his car . . . you needn't put a tail on him."

"Thanks," Steve grinned. "Does that mean I'm scratched off your list of suspects?"

"No." Duveen's expression was bleak. "It means I'm trusting you to come back here, that's all. If you don't . . . if I have to send somebody after you . . . well, you won't be living at a hotel any longer . . . is that clear?"

"As a bell," Steve replied. "A whole chime of bells, in fact. Don't worry. I'll be back all right. So long."

XII

There was just time, Steve found, to stop for a bite of lunch, before keeping his appointment with Dr. Badouine at two o'clock.

He ascended the steps of the large, old-fashioned house on K Street, hopeful, but by no means optimistic.

It was very possible that the doctor, having treated Mrs. Kirby during her recent nervous breakdown, might know something of her enemies, her fears. Whether professional ethics would prevent him from discussing such matters, in a search for possible murder motives, was another question.

Steve gave his name to the crisply starched secretary, followed her into the consulting room, not over-sanguine.

Dr. Badouine's greeting, however, his firm, friendly handshake, somewhat reassured him.

"Glad to see you, Mr. Ransom," he said, pointing to a chair. "Sit down. And tell me the latest news about poor Mrs. Kirby's death. Have the police discovered any worthwhile clues?"

Steve mentioned the penholder, the results of the post-mortem, the dead hairs found in the murdered woman's fingers, the discovery of the pearls, repeating the Inspector's caution that the latter bit of evidence was not to be given to the newspapers. So far as the snapshot found on the desk was concerned, the doctor had seen that, or at least a part of it, the night before.

"Apparently," Steve concluded, "the woman who came to the house last night must have worn a wig and was thus not necessarily a brunette. Nor, for that matter, not necessarily a woman. As for the pearls, Inspector Duveen thinks they were planted . . . a false clue."

"But why?"

"Well, everyone knew Mrs. Kirby was wearing a necklace during the evening. Miss Vickery, the servants, so testified . . . thought it the real string. Suppose it was. Then the murderer got the genuine pearls and left the phony ones in their place."

"What good would that do, if the real string is missing?"

"But it isn't missing. That's just the point. Miss Kirby has it. Says her mother gave her the necklace yesterday afternoon. To take care of. She might be saying that to protect de Zara; they were together, she says, at his apartment. I don't accuse the girl, of course. Certainly not of anything more than trying to help her sweetheart. But whoever took those fake pearls from Mrs. Kirby's bedroom, hid them in the flower vase, must have been someone inside the house, and since it wasn't Miss Vickery . . ."

"You feel sure of that, do you?"

"Of course!"

The doctor shook his head, a faint smile about his eyes.

"When do you think Miss Kirby could have done it?" he asked.

"Why . . . this morning sometime . . ."

"Haven't you forgotten that one of the imitation pearls was found on the floor last night?"

"That's so." Steve laughed, a bit foolishly.

"Then the things must have been planted in the vase last night."

Again Dr. Badouine smiled.

"Isn't it much more reasonable," he said, "to believe that Mrs. Kirby was wearing the imitation string when she was killed? And that the murderer, discovering they were of no value, simply tossed them into the vase?"

"How could he discover that so quickly? They'd fool the average person . . . unless he had a chance to compare them . . ."

"Possibly our murderer is not an average person. And there is also the chance that Mrs. Kirby on finding she was about to be choked, may have tried to save herself by muttering something to the effect that the string was not genuine."

"In which case we have to suppose that a desperate killer, in a hurry to escape, would take the trouble to pick up all those pearls from the floor and put them in the vase. He only missed one, you remember. Which proves the string was broken. I still think the whole thing a plant."

"You may be right." The doctor nodded. "But if so, I am afraid it looks rather bad for Miss Vickery."

"Nonsense!" Steve exclaimed, very red.

Dr. Badouine gazed across the glass-topped desk, his clever face no longer smiling.

"You have asked my help, Mr. Ransom," he said gravely, "and I am trying to give it to you; my remarks are not meant to be personal. We know Miss Vickery was in the house at the time of the murder. And we know Miss Kirby was not . . ."

"How do we know she wasn't? First she claims to have been driving about. Now she says she was with de Zara, at his apartment. I don't believe she had anything to do with the murder . . . that would be absurd. But she may have been the tall woman who came to the house around eleven o'clock! Suppose she had reason to think de Zara might have done the killing, or was in danger of becoming involved in it! Couldn't she have picked up those pearls, dropped them in the vase, to throw suspicion on somebody else? And then ran out, just before I got there?"

Dr. Badouine asked a slow, deliberate question.

"On whom did it throw suspicion, so far as the police are concerned?"

"Why . . . on Miss Vickery . . . damn it."

"There you are. That is why I suggested the danger of insisting that the pearls were a plant. I still believe they were placed where you found them by the murderer. And if the fact of their having been picked up from the floor seems unreasonable, assuming he knew they were valueless, then we are forced to conclude that he . . . or she . . . did *not* know that, and hid the pearls in the flower vase supposing them to be real, and expecting to recover them at his . . . or her . . . leisure."

Steve Ransom ground his cigarette into an ash tray, frowning. This, he remembered, was precisely the line of argument Inspector Duveen had employed, in questioning Ann. It seemed logical enough . . . horribly so! And taken in connection with the girl's orders to move the vase from the room that morning . . .

"Look here, doctor," he said. "What I hoped to get from you was a possible reason for Mrs. Kirby's death. Motive. Can you, from your knowledge of her . . . ah . . . troubles, suggest one?"

Dr. Badouine sat drumming his well-kept fingers on the desk-top.

"I spoke last night of Mrs. Kirby's dislike for Count de Zara," he replied. "I may even say, without going too far, her hatred; it amounted to that. But whether de Zara hated Mrs. Kirby, strongly enough to kill her, is of course beyond my knowledge. I understand you saw him, and talked with him this morning. What is your opinion?"

"I don't know. He seemed very much upset."

"Naturally. And what was it you learned from him that caused you to suspect this actor, Dane?"

"Why, something de Zara told me about the photograph."

"Photograph?" the doctor asked vaguely.

"Yes. The one Duveen showed you last night."

"Oh . . . that!" Dr. Badouine smiled. "To be exact, I was shown only half of it."

"Well, you've seen more than I have," Steve said. "Duveen isn't taking anybody into his confidence, on that subject. But I do know the picture belonged to de Zara; he kept it locked in a box at his apartment, a sort of steel casket."

"Then," the doctor said sharply, "if, as I assume from Inspector Duveen's questions last night, it was found on the scene of the crime, how does de Zara explain its presence?"

"He says someone stole the picture from his studio, during a party he gave there not long ago. Dane was one of the guests."

"Easy to say." Dr. Badouine's expression was cynical. "So you went to see Dane? What did you find out from him?"

"Nothing very definite. He'd been up most of the night, was nervous, jittery . . . whether from being grilled by the police, or too much White Label Scotch I couldn't tell. That boy sure can punish his liquor; buys it by the case, he says. However, he did let out a word or two that made me feel he knew something about the photograph."

"How so?"

"Well, when I mentioned the fact that it might have been stolen, he said, to protect himself, no doubt, that anyone could have taken it from the box. And the funny part was, that up to then I hadn't told him de Zara kept the picture in a box. So you see . . ."

"Yes." The doctor nodded. "And what do you conclude?"

"Either that Dane saw someone else steal the picture, or took it himself!"

"I see. Very likely." Dr. Badouine got up, began to pace the floor, his head bent. "Now we are getting somewhere. What does Inspector Duveen think of this? I consider him a man of unusual ability."

"I don't know. As soon as I mentioned the picture he blew up. Afraid, as I told you, that some word of it might get to the newspapers."

"I can understand that . . . assuming the photograph may have involved Mrs. Kirby or her daughter. The Senator would be a dangerous man to antagonize. But to come back to Dane. If he stole the picture he may be the murderer."

"And if he didn't steal it," Steve added quickly, "but knows who did, he will probably, now that I've put him wise to the importance of the matter, go straight to the police!"

"Do you think so? Not necessarily. Suppose, for instance, he saw Senator Kirby take the photograph? I happen to know," the doctor added, with his quick, comprehending smile, "that the Senator was a guest at that party, for I was there myself. And I also know, and feel free to say so, that he, Senator Kirby, has been trying for some time to find evidence to enable him to secure a divorce. Possibly he decided to look for it, in de Zara's souvenir casket."

"And having found it," Steve muttered, "promptly murdered his wife!"

"That is a possibility, we must admit. You see, I happen to know that Mrs. Kirby and de Zara met abroad. And while I have seen only half the snapshot in question, I could not help reading part of a tender love-message written across the bottom of it. Senator Kirby is a man of violent temper. If he thought his wife had been carrying on an affair with de Zara, he might have killed her, in a fit of rage."

"Exactly. But you started to tell me why you think Dane, if he saw Kirby take the picture, wouldn't tell the police."

"That is elemental. By going to the police, he will gain nothing, except a little cheap notoriety. By going to Senator Kirby, he might possibly sell his silence for a very large sum."

"Of course," Steve muttered, "of course! Stupid of me not to think of it. You sure do know human nature, doctor."

"At least some phases of it . . . not always the pleasantest phases, either. But we must not allow Senator Kirby's hatred of his wife to run away with our judgment. Mrs. Kirby herself had every reason to want to obtain possession of that photograph."

"But Mrs. Kirby wasn't at de Zara's party."

"I know. But her lawyer, Judge Tyson, was."

"Good Lord!" Steve gasped. "I remember now de Zara said the judge was there. Maybe Dane saw *him* take the picture!"

"In which case," the doctor went on, smiling, "our clever but penurious actor would be in an even better position. Mrs. Kirby is . . . was . . . an extremely wealthy woman."

"That might account for the bonds," Steve muttered.

"Bonds? What bonds?" The doctor paused in his pacing.

"Oh, a couple of hundred thousand dollars' worth, found in Mrs. Kirby's safe; it seems she got them from the bank sometime yesterday. What I mean is, supposing Dane, instead of seeing someone else take the picture, stole it himself, he may have gone there to the house and for some reason killed her. Only, I can't quite see what she meant about that nail."

"Nail?" Dr. Badouine asked quickly. "I'm afraid I don't follow you."

"Just before Mrs. Kirby was killed, Miss Vickery, who occupied the suite above, heard her cry out something that sounded like 'The nail!' or 'That nail!'"

Dr. Badouine stood staring at his desk-top with a somewhat puzzled smile.

"Afraid I can't help you, there," he said. "It doesn't make much sense, does it? Unless," he added suddenly, "what Miss Vickery heard was not 'That nail,' but 'Blackmail.' After all, the two do sound very much alike."

Steve jumped from his chair.

"You've got it!" he exclaimed. "Blackmail! And whoever the blackmailer was, he undoubtedly killed her, before she could alarm the house! Probably Dane! He must have stolen the photograph himself!"

"Certainly," Dr. Badouine agreed, "he had the opportunity; de Zara left the box open for an hour or more, to my personal knowledge, after getting out his Napoleonic letter."

"Of course there were others who had a similar opportunity," Steve suggested, "and might have wanted the photograph, too, as we've just said. Judge Tyson, Senator Kirby, Luke Reed, and a woman with him whose name I don't know. There was also an actress who came with Dane . . ."

"True." The doctor nodded. "But Dane's chances were much better than the others."

"Why?"

"Because, while de Zara was playing, singing his Dalmatian songs, we all were gathered about the piano; all, that is, except Dane. He spent a great deal of time in the front part of the room where the bar was. I couldn't see him, because of an intervening screen . . . didn't try to, in fact. Having heard he was a heavy drinker, I naturally concluded that he preferred highballs to de Zara's musical efforts, but now you have told me about the missing photograph, his actions become significant."

"I'll say they do!" Steve agreed. "Just how, doctor, would you reconstruct the crime?"

"Well," Dr. Badouine said, sinking back into his chair, "I lay no claims to special knowledge in such matters, but as a guess why not something like this? Dane, we all know, used to be a fairly prominent actor. Circumstances have reduced him to playing small parts in stock, at a small salary. He needs money, knows from being a visitor at the house, that there is trouble between Mrs. Kirby and her husband. When the Count opened his souvenir box, Dane noticed there were letters, photographs, in it. At the first opportunity he investigated, saw the snapshot, took it, meaning to make use of the thing, inscribed with its tender message in Mrs. Kirby's handwriting, to extort money from her. Went to the house last night disguised as a woman . . . not a difficult matter for an actor of his general appearance and build. When his demands caused his victim to cry out that she was being blackmailed he first choked, then killed her, fearing if he didn't she would have him arrested on what, as you know, is an extremely serious criminal charge. No doubt he left the photograph behind hoping to involve de Zara."

"But the bonds," Steve objected. "I still can't see why, if Mrs. Kirby had them there to pay over to Dane in return for the picture, she should have been surprised . . . should have cried out that she was being blackmailed. She knew that already."

"Then the only logical conclusion would seem to be," the doctor replied, "that she had these bonds there for some other and entirely different purpose. Possibly to pay to de Zara, as a bribe for not marrying her daughter."

"Might be." Steve sat staring at his cigarette. "One thing is certain; if her visitor was a man, in disguise, it wasn't de Zara. That heavyweight couldn't make up to look like a woman in a million years. But why would Dane do it? Disguise himself, I mean?"

"Possibly to avoid being recognized by the servants."

"Possibly. But there is a chance that instead of a man in disguise Mrs. Kirby's caller might really have been a woman. The red-headed ex-maid, for instance, with her carrot-top hid under a wig. Easy enough to open the French window, let de Zara in to do the killing."

"Except for his alibi."

"Yes." Steve nodded. "It does look as if Dane was our meat. Any objection to my telling Inspector Duveen what you've just said about his stealing that picture?"

"I didn't see him steal it, remember. Merely suggested that he had an excellent opportunity."

"But you didn't notice anyone else near the box?"

"No . . . not that I remember."

"Well, then . . . what more do you want?"

"To be a little surer of my ground." Dr. Badouine smiled across the desk at Steve, his eyes very warm and human. "Both as a physician and a man, I prefer not to indulge in careless statements. Dane may be guilty, I am afraid he is, but we ought to avoid hasty conclusions . . . give him the benefit of every possible doubt. Before the police take any action, I should very much like to talk with him."

"I see," Steve grinned. "A little psycho-analysis."

"Call it that, if you wish. At any rate, without being conceited, I do think that my experience as a psychiatrist could be put to some helpful use. A few questions might enable me to find out what, if anything, he really knows about Mrs. Kirby's death."

"I'd guess plenty from the way he acted with me this morning. And the minute I tell the Inspector what you've said it's a safe bet he'll have Dane brought in at once, if only for a shellacking."

"Then don't tell him. Or if you do, ask him not to make an arrest until tomorrow. That will give us an opportunity to see Dane tonight. I suggest that you call him up and make an engagement for after the performance . . . say we'll stop by and take him to supper."

"We."

"Of course. Naturally I'm counting on your co-operation. And I rather think, after your talk with him this morning, he'll be more likely to meet you, than he would me alone, if only to find out what you know about that photograph. It may even scare him a little, assuming of course that he is guilty. Make him talk. Nothing like an uneasy conscience, and a few drinks, to loosen a man's tongue. When shall I meet you? Half past ten?"

"Too late. Better make it ten o'clock. At the theatre. Dane isn't on in the last act, which is another reason I'm suspicious of him. No alibi, after ten-twenty or thereabouts. Ample time to put on a disguise, get out to Halfway House by a little after eleven . . ."

"At ten o'clock, then." The doctor put out his hand. "In the lobby. And remember, while this playing at detective work may be amusing, I am first of all a physician. My job is not to hurt, but to heal. So tell your Inspector to keep his bloodhounds off until we see if we can't help Mr. Dane. He may have something on his conscience that is worrying him. Most of my time is spent persuading my patients to get rid of such knowledge, to drag it out into the light, where it can no longer do them harm."

"Right," Steve said. "I'm not trying to hurt the poor guy either. But if he's guilty he'll have to suffer for it, I guess. Thanks a lot, doctor. See you at ten!"

XIII

Steve, telling his story to Duveen at Halfway House, did not find the Inspector greatly impressed.

"Guesswork, most of it," he said. "Just a chance Dane may have taken the picture, but no proof. See if you can't dig up some facts. I don't mind telling you" . . . Duveen was thinking of the half-burned correspondence card with Lawrence Dane's name on it which had been found in the fireplace . . . "that I was about set to ask that bird a few questions myself. But tomorrow's time enough; right now I'm investigating a couple of other angles."

"The doctor and I may get something," Steve said. "I want to see the case settled if only so Miss Vickery and I can go home."

"You're doing pretty well, young fellow, right here in Washington." Duveen gave a chuckle. "The lady was asking me not ten minutes ago how soon you'd be back. Why don't you check out at the hotel, and bunk in here for a day or two . . . until after the inquest, at any rate. That will give me a chance to keep an eye on you and give you a chance to be with your girl friend. It's okey with the Senator, I asked him."

"Is that an order?" Steve grinned.

"Take it as one, if it'll help."

"Help? Say, Inspector, you're the top! I'll speak to Senator Kirby about the matter right now."

Steve left the Inspector sitting in the morning room and went down the long corridor toward the west wing of the house. He was thinking, not of the murder, but of Ann Vickery.

A great kid. Straight and fine as they made them. Even Duveen saw that; his suspicions of the girl appeared rather half-hearted. Of course, as an efficient police officer he was bound to follow up all leads, but nobody, however cynical, could look at Ann and believe her capable of a brutal, cold-blooded murder. At least *he* couldn't. Rather absurd, to bring up the point that she had once been a student nurse. Trained nurses weren't any more hard or cruel than other women; they were merely taught to be more efficient, to keep their emotions under control. He felt sure that Ann had plenty, behind her cool, direct eyes, her challenging smile.

The door of Senator Kirby's study was closed. A deep, oratorical voice answered the knock.

"Come!" it said.

Steve went into the room. Senator Kirby was bent over a carved oak desk, writing. His eyes were hollow from loss of sleep and his gaunt, bony face made one think of a dead Pharaoh.

"I'm told by Inspector Duveen," Steve said, "that I'm to stay here at your house for a day or two, until this dreadful affair has been cleared up. He wants me as a witness, at the inquest, and says he has your permission."

"Yes." The Senator peered through his ragged grey eyebrows.

"I'm sorry, of course, to trouble you . . ."

"My permission ceases, young man, when you *do* trouble me. By talking too much. Or interfering in matters which are none of your concern. That is all." The Senator resumed his writing.

"Charming host!" Steve muttered, as he went out to the garden. Three women were coming toward him across the smoothly clipped lawn; in the afternoon sunlight they cast long, wavering shadows.

Jean Kirby was one. The short, blonde woman beside her he recognized as Mrs. Conover, whom he had met the afternoon before. The other figure was Ann.

"How do you do," Steve said, embarrassed. "I find, Miss Kirby, that at Inspector Duveen's orders I am to be a guest here, in your house. I sincerely regret . . ."

"It . . . it's quite all right, Mr. Ransom." The girl's voice was as pale, as devoid of color as her cheeks. "Edward will see to it; I'll speak to him."

"Please don't trouble."

"Let me, dear." Mrs. Conover laid her hand on the girl's arm. "You run along and lie down for a while; I'll come and rub your head." She watched Jean go into the house, walking like a somnambulist. "Hasn't closed her eyes all day; she'll break down if she doesn't get some sleep. Did you and Dr. Badouine find out anything?" She turned to Steve. "He told me you were coming to see him."

"Nothing definite," Steve said. "We're meeting again, tonight. By the way, Mrs. Conover, I believe you attended a party at Count de Zara's studio not long ago."

"Why, yes." The woman seemed surprised. "Jean suggested it. The doctor took me. Nick wanted to show us his collection of pistols and things."

"He also showed you, didn't he, a valuable letter?"

"Yes. Written by Napoleon, I believe. From Malta, or Elba, or some such place; I wasn't particularly interested . . . everybody writes letters . . . too many, mostly. Glad I haven't the habit." She glanced down at her small, heavily ringed hands, smiling enigmatically.

"Did you notice where he kept the letter?" Steve asked.

"I certainly did. In the loveliest box. Inlaid with gold. Like a queen's jewel casket. And filled with old pictures and whatnot. Trophies of the chase, de Zara calls them; well, I wouldn't say so to Jean but I'll bet he's done plenty of chasing. What's your interest? If you're thinking of buying the box I can tell you now he won't sell it; I asked him."

"No. I wasn't." Steve, meeting Mrs. Conover's vivacious eyes, noticed the tiny network of wrinkles surrounding them. A very attractive woman, but not so young in the sunshine, as under a kinder light. "I merely wondered if you remember any of the other guests at the party standing about that inlaid box, taking particular interest in it."

Mrs. Conover thought, regarding her scarlet finger tips.

"Of course I wouldn't be likely to, after all this time," she said. "I recollect we had some bad music . . . Nick's *forte* should be moving pianos, not playing them . . . and some worse whiskey . . . Mr. Reed wouldn't drink it."

"You mean Luke Reed? Senator Kirby's lawyer?"

"Certainly. I always feel like giving the 'View Halloo' whenever I see him. If Nature hadn't forgotten a tail, he'd have been a perfect fox."

"Do you remember a rather large, handsome woman who came with him?"

"If you mean Mrs. Mitchell, I certainly do. Only I shouldn't call Babs handsome exactly. I mean *I* shouldn't. Looks too much like a horse for my taste. And I shouldn't say she came with Mr. Reed, either, as long as Senator Kirby was in the party."

"And just what am I to understand from that?"

"Suit yourself; it depends on how suspicious a nature you have. Only Luke Reed is a cast-iron bachelor; wouldn't marry the best woman on earth, he says, which certainly let's Babs out. And of course, when a prominent statesman uses his lawyer as a chaperon, I have my thoughts." Mrs.

Conover's slanting, oriental eyes narrowed impishly. "Now that you speak of it, Babs . . . Mrs. Mitchell; she's a widow . . . grass . . . and anxious to repeat . . . was interested in that jewel box of Nick's, too. I saw her showing Mr. Reed the inlaid coat-of-arms on the lid, telling him she'd adore to have one like it to keep her love-letters in; personally I doubt if a trunk would be big enough. Well, I must go rub poor Jean's head. Bye."

Ann looked after her, smiling.

"Nice pussy," she. said. "Shall we sit down? Or are you too busy?"

"Haven't a thing to do until I meet Dr. Badouine at ten o'clock; that gives us the rest of the afternoon, and half of the evening."

"For what?" Ann looked up expectantly; she was thinking how little time they had had with each other, so far.

"My suggestion would be dinner. In town somewhere. And a few spots of dancing, afterwards."

"Do you think the Inspector will let us go?"

"We'll ask him. After all, this isn't our tragedy, even if we have been dragged into it. I think you need to get your mind off the thing for a while."

Inspector Duveen, whom they found in the morning room, received their request with a cryptic smile.

"Sure," he said, regarding Steve shrewdly. "That will give you a chance, young fellow, to check out, at your hotel. Bring your suitcase, if you've got one, back here."

"I hope so," Steve said. "I wired for it."

"You people better use the back way," Duveen went on. "There's a mob of news hounds and camera men out front. I'll have one of the boys bring your car around." He left them, went down the hall.

Steve crossed the room, stood looking at the Della Robbia plaque that hid the wall-safe. It still stood open.

"You can't even see the hinges," Ann said.

"No. To look at it, you'd think it was just set in the plaster. Stonework, I mean." He clicked the plaque shut. "Now how do you open the thing?"

Ann ran her fingers along the edge of the bit of terra cotta work, projecting a quarter of an inch beyond the smooth surface of the chimney breast.

"There's a little metal catch here," she whispered, pressing it. At once the plaque swung open.

Steve examined the small, bright bit of metal; it strongly resembled the circular head of a large wire nail.

"Maybe," he said, "but I doubt it. I think we're all wet, about that nail business. Dr. Badouine has the right idea."

"What?" Ann asked.

"He thinks what Mrs. Kirby called out just before her death was 'Blackmail.'"

"It's an idea," Ann said. "Rather a good one."

Inspector Duveen came in from the hall.

"All set!" he announced. "Go out through the garden. And look here, you two, remember we've got a pretty good detective force here in Washington. We're working on a lot of angles you don't know anything about. Stop worrying about this terrible affair and enjoy yourselves." His smile, while amiable, was a bit frosty.

Ann glanced at Steve, her eyes crinkling.

"I can think of lots of things I'd rather talk about," she said, "than murders."

XIV

The hotel dining room, in spite of its smartly dressed crowd offered no facilities for dancing, but Steve, with a ten o'clock engagement ahead of him decided there was not time to hunt up a gayer place. He glanced across the table at Ann, sipping her *demi tasse*.

"Not like other girls," he said slowly.

Ann's head snapped up.

"I hope that ancient wheeze," she retorted, "doesn't imply any essential lack . . ."

"Only the grin . . ."

"What grin?"

"The usual dental ad one. You know. All set to bite. What sharp teeth you have, Grandmother. Great mistake, I think. You've been sitting opposite me for almost two hours and haven't done it once. Anyway, who wants to kiss a flock of teeth?"

"I didn't know anything had been said about kissing."

"Do I have to call my shots? I've been thinking about it ever since we met."

"What a strain. Twenty-four hours. I wonder you can stand it."

"Months, beautiful. Years. Ages."

"The old 'where have you been all my life?' stuff. I expected better of you. Yesterday morning you didn't even know I existed."

"And tonight I'm buying dinner for you. We live in a swift-moving age, darling. Who knows what new and even more delightful experience may be waiting for us, just around the corner?"

Ann deliberately grinned; her small, even teeth were very white and lovely.

"A lot of people," she said, "have slipped up, predicting what was just around that corner. Who, for instance, would have expected to run across a murder?"

"I thought we weren't going to talk about the murder."

"You might find it more exciting."

"Impossible!" Steve shook his head. "In that respect you're the top, angel. I know."

Ann's long, almond-shaped eyes, drooping slightly at the corners, made her look almost oriental.

"You don't know anything about me," she said, "except that I'm an interior decorator."

"I don't even know that, except from what you've told me. Any more than you know I'm a playwright. In fact, from some of the things the critics said about my recent opus, it's a matter of doubt."

"Which makes the score fifty-fifty. Neither of us has anything to live up . . . or down . . . to. We take each other as is."

"For better or worse." Steve grinned across the table. "I'm all for that."

"In other words, we start from scratch."

"No handicaps, in the way of husbands, fiancés?"

"None. And you?"

"Not even a rich uncle, ready to die and leave me a million. I have to work for my champagne and caviar."

"Same here."

"Which makes us just a couple of poor but honest proletarians, doing our best to get along. What could be sweeter? Nothing between us but . . . love . . . ."

"And a murder."

"That's twice you've come back to it. Why?"

Ann crumpled her cigarette in the coffee saucer; her keen, sensitive face was suddenly grave.

"Because it *is* there, facing us . . . will be, until the murderer is discovered. You've been awfully decent about it, but the fact remains that you don't really know I didn't kill Mrs. Kirby."

"Oh, yes I do."

"How."

"The same way I know there are such things as cosmic rays, and the force of gravity, and the North Pole. I've never seen any of them . . . don't have to. We take things like that on faith. That's the way I feel about you. Right?"

"You're sweet," Ann said. "And I feel the same way about you. But other people don't. Inspector Duveen, for one. He's been very nice, but if it hadn't been for that photograph he found under Mrs. Kirby's head we'd both of us be locked up right now. And if he can find any reasonable explanation of its being there, apart from the murder, we will be."

"Yes," Steve said uneasily, running his fingers through his cinnamon brown hair. "I know it. But after the doctor and I see Lawrence Dane tonight . . ."

"Has it occurred to you," Ann whispered, "that Mr. Dane might give that reasonable explanation. Suppose he should admit having stolen that photograph! Suppose he should say Mrs. Kirby asked him to steal it? They were old friends. Suppose he should say he gave it to her yesterday, after the luncheon party, saw her put it in her desk! Then where would we be?"

"In the cooler." Steve laughed, not a happy laugh. "Although at that, I can't see what she was doing with it, when she was killed."

"Neither can I. Showing it to somebody, perhaps. What do you think of de Zara?" Ann suddenly asked.

"Not a bad guy. He struck me as being straightforward, sincere. Nothing to speak of, under the brainpan, but very much in love with Jean Kirby. Why?"

Ann was tracing intricate designs on the table cloth.

"Don't turn around," she said softly, "but he's sitting three tables behind you, in the corner. With a slender, dark woman who looks like a foreigner. French, perhaps, or Italian. They are both jabbering away excitedly and haven't seen us."

Steve's shoulders stiffened, but he did not turn until the arrival of the waiter with the check gave him an excuse to do so.

"De Zara, all right," he muttered, when the man had gone. "The woman's a stranger. Nothing to it, I guess; only a fool would appear with his accomplice, in public."

"A fool . . . or a very clever man. Ordinarily, after what has happened, I should not have expected to see him in public, with a woman, at all. But I suppose, leading a studio existence, he has to dine out somewhere. Why not with a friend? Be careful . . . they're going now."

As the Count and his companion reached the main doorway he turned and caught sight of Steve and Ann. With a word to the woman, he came across the room, smiling, bent over their table.

"This is nice," he murmured, kissing Ann's hand. "How are you, Mr. Ransom? And my poor Jean? You will say that you met me, yes . . . and give her my love? Tonight I ask for dinner the wife of an old friend, from New York; she speaks no English, so I did not bring her to meet you. Now I must take her to the train." He fumbled like a shy and overgrown schoolboy with the paper-wrapped package he carried. "Some refreshment for her, on the journey, you understand. A little wine. Abroad, we do not understand the quaint American custom of drinking water. Now, you will excuse, it is necessary to make the hurry, or her train may depart." He bowed stiffly from the waist in continental fashion, was gone.

Steve glanced at his watch.

"We'll have to be moving ourselves, sweetness," he said quickly. "It's after nine. Sorry about those dances but we'll make up for it another time. I've got to check out here, take you to Halfway House, be back at the theatre to meet Dr. Badouine at ten. Anyway, we'll have time for a little drive together. Maybe I'll find those kisses I've been thinking about just around the corner."

Ann got up. Once more her lips curled in a round and stereotyped grin.

"The better to bite you with, my dear," she said.

"Wuff . . . wuff!" Steve grinned back at her. The expression in Ann's eyes stopped him.

"Not like other girls," she went on steadily.

"Not even . . . around the corner?"

Ann Vickery began to laugh.

"There are lots of girls," she said, "and lots of corners. Better be sure both are the right ones, before you do anything rash."

XV

There was no one in the lobby of the theatre when Steve reached it at ten o'clock, but a moment later Dr. Badouine joined him.

"Was afraid I'd be late," the doctor said. "Had to stop for oil and gas." He looked at Steve, smiling. "Were you successful in making an engagement with Mr. Dane?"

"Didn't try. Just left a note at his hotel saying I'd be around after the second act, to see him about something important."

"You didn't mention, then, that you were bringing me?"

"No. I thought it might scare him. We'll just say I ran into you, after the first intermission, and brought you along for a drink or something."

"Too bad," the doctor said, a gleam of humor in his eyes, "that I haven't seen the play. If Mr. Dane is like most actors, the surest way to gain his confidence, induce him to talk, is to tell him how much I enjoyed his acting."

Steve looked at his watch.

"Ten-five. This act rings down about ten-twenty, if I remember correctly; that will give us fifteen minutes to watch his work. He's the whole show, in this particular scene; if you butter him up on that, he won't think about the rest of the performance. Wait; I'll buy a couple of admission; we can stand back, until the curtain's down."

The theatre was not crowded. Steve thought he saw Senator Kirby's lawyer, Luke Reed, with a party in one of the lower boxes, but couldn't be sure. He and the doctor hung over the rail, watching the act draw to its climax. Lawrence Dane, in the part of a brilliant but unscrupulous criminal lawyer, was arranging to sell out one of his clients, a boy accused of murder, in return for certain political advantages; he carried the scene well.

"I shouldn't think, to look at him now," Dr. Badouine whispered, "that he was a man who did much drinking."

"He doesn't," Steve whispered back, "before performances. I've always heard that about Dane. He's what they call 'a good trouper.' But you can bet his first move when he gets back to his dressing room, will be to knock off a couple of Scotch highballs."

"Can't say I blame him much," Dr. Badouine was watching the stage. "Rather a trying part, I should imagine."

"It is. This scene, anyway; he hasn't a great deal to do, in the rest of the play. Dane's a fine actor. Used to be, at least. A little old-fashioned, now, for the current Broadway taste."

The scene was progressing rapidly, building up to its sudden and unexpected climax . . . a climax in which Dane, the lawyer, having completed his deal at the cost of his client's life, tells a woman about it . . . the woman with whom he is living . . . mentions, in an unguarded moment, the victim's name.

Steve turned to the doctor.

"If you had seen the first part of the show," he said, "you'd understand this better. The dame with the brassy top-piece is the accused boy's sister."

"Yes, I know," the doctor nodded. "Obviously there must be some such connection. Now what does she do?"

"You'll see," Steve whispered, grinning.

What the brassy-haired lady did was to snatch a pistol from her dressing-table and shoot the lawyer through the heart.

"Well, that's that!" Steve was yawning. "Not a bad finish, for an act." The curtain came down to vigorous applause, rose again for curtain calls. Steve and the doctor strolled out to the lobby, now beginning to fill as smokers hurried from their seats. "Might as well have a cigarette, before we go back stage; give Dane time to shed his make-up," Steve said. "How about you?" He held out his case.

"Thanks." The doctor shook his head. "Not one of my vices. If I had a wife," he went on, laughing, "I suppose she would want me to explain that statement; luckily, being a bachelor, I don't have to."

Steve lit a cigarette.

"Just what line are you going to take with Dane?" he asked.

"Why, my idea was that you should tell him you're certain he knows who stole that photograph, and want his help. Then we'll see what he has to say. The fact that I am present will worry him considerably, because he will remember me as having also been a guest at de Zara's party, and he can't be sure how much I know. He may even think I saw him take the picture."

"Then you aren't going to ask him a lot of questions?"

"He'll probably tell us what we want without being asked, in an effort to clear himself. That's human nature. Human psychology. A person will say much more, if you create in his mind the fear that you know something already. He will almost inevitably try to correct, to alter what he fears may be an unfavorable impression."

Steve tossed away his cigarette, pushed open the door to the street.

"Come along," he said.

They followed the sidewalk to the narrow alley leading to the stage entrance. The grey old man at the door peered at them over his glasses.

"I'm Stephen Ransom, the playwright," Steve said. "This gentleman and I have an appointment with Mr. Dane. Lawrence Dane."

"In his dressing room," the doorkeeper mumbled. "Number 3. Up them steps." He waved toward an iron staircase.

Steve went first; he was familiar with the world back stage.

"Mr. Dane!" he called, rapping briskly on the door of the dressing room. "It's Ransom! Steve Ransom!"

There was no response. Steve rapped again, then pushed the door wide.

"Good God!" he gasped, horrified.

Lawrence Dane, in his undershirt, lolled over the arm of a chair. His mouth hung open, horribly open; on the top of a trunk stood a glass and two bottles, one of liquor, the other, brown and slender necked, containing soda. Both were nearly full. Steve noticed these small details in the moment it took the doctor to reach Dane's side.

"He's dead!" Dr. Badouine exclaimed, straightening up. "Looks as though he'd been poisoned! What a horrible situation! You'd better call the police!"

XVI

Steve dashed from the dressing room, ran down the steps to the stage entrance. Lawrence Dane dead! Poisoned, perhaps! It was incredible! Only a few moments ago they had seen him leave the stage! The man they so certainly believed to be Mrs. Kirby's murderer! Well . . . he could still be that . . . guilty men before now had dodged the gallows by the suicide route. Yet, for suicide, it seemed strangely premature; so far Dane had not even been accused of anything.

"Telephone?" Steve called to the doorkeeper.

The man blinked at him, annoyed.

"You shouldn't shout like that, young fellow," he admonished. "They'll hear you on stage. If you want to telephone you'll have to go round front, or to the drugstore across the street."

Steve raced on, down the alley. Although, his brain told him, there was no need for such great haste, now. If Dane had killed himself . . .

At the mouth of the alley a figure loomed against the street lights. A tall man, in plain clothes; Steve thought he had seen him before.

"What's your hurry, Mr. Ransom?" he asked. Then, misunderstanding the look of alarm on Steve's face, he added; "Inspector Duveen told me to keep an eye on you, see you didn't get into any trouble. Been talking to Dane?"

"Dane," Steve muttered, "is dead! Dr. Badouine and I just found him . . ."

"What?" The detective fought against the absurdity of the idea; he, too, had been standing out front, had watched the actor respond to a curtain call not ten minutes before. "Say, don't kid me!"

"You'd better come and see for yourself!" Steve said. "I was going to telephone the Inspector!"

The man ran up the alley, charged past the astonished doorkeeper without a word. For a moment he spoke to the policeman back stage, then turned to Steve.

"Show me where this guy's dressing room is," he said. "And . . . wait a minute!" He beckoned to the door-keeper. "Come here, Pop! Now get this! I'm from Head-quarters . . . detective bureau, see? There's some trouble back stage. You don't let anybody in or out until the Inspector shows up, understand? Inspector Duveen. I've just sent that cop to telephone for him. When he gets back, he'll stick around with you. At the door. You needn't give any alarm just yet, get me? Keep your trap shut . . . the show should be over in twenty minutes . . . half an hour. Right." He turned to Steve. "Now where's Dane?"

They went up the stairs; the doctor was standing at the door of the dressing room.

"This is Dr. Badouine," Steve said.

"Yes, I know." The detective nodded, went inside. "Was he just like this when you found him?" he asked, staring down at Dane's limp body.

"Just like that." Dr. Badouine replied. "Except to feel his pulse, we haven't touched anything. He was dead, when we arrived. While it is only a guess I should say, in the absence of any visible wound that he'd been poisoned."

"Looks like it." The plain-clothes man inspected the two bottles, the glass, without touching them. "No trouble to tell, I guess, as soon as we have these analyzed." The whiskey bottle was almost full, and so was that containing the soda; the outside of the latter showed a film of moisture, condensed in tiny beads. There was perhaps a teaspoonful of pale liquid in the bottom of the glass.

"He can't have been dead over four or five minutes," Dr. Badouine continued. "Some quick-acting poison such as potassium cyanide, I venture to say. Anything slower, taken before he went on the stage, would almost certainly have made him ill during the performance; as far as I could see, he acted quite normally, until the curtain fell."

The plain-clothes man pointed to the large bottle of soda.

"That ain't been off the ice ten minutes," he said. "Notice the sweat on the glass. So somebody must have brought it." He went to the top of the stairs, shouted down to the doorkeeper. "Hey, Pop . . . how'd Mr. Dane get the bottle of soda?"

"One of the call boys . . ."

"Send him up here, quick!"

The detective waited until the boy came to the top of the stairs; he did not let him see into the room.

"You got Mr. Dane some soda?"

"Yep. Quart. Across the street."

"When?"

"Just now. When he came off stage after the second act. He gave me two bits, said to have it cold and hurry; he needed a high-ball!"

"You take it into his room? This room?"

"Yep. Opened it for him. He had a corkscrew in his knife, but gentlemen in his day, he said didn't carry can openers; that's a stock joke of his . . . he springs it on me every night."

"Oh, then you got him soda every night, eh?"

"Sure. Regular. And opened it for him." The boy took a metal implement from his pocket.

"Ever take a drink with him?"

"No."

"Didn't, eh? Why not?"

"He never ast me."

"All right. So you opened the soda. What then?"

"Mr. Dane came across the room; he'd been washing the glass at the basin over there . . . poured himself a shot of liquor, filled it up with soda, and started to drink it."

"And what did you do?"

"I went out and shut the door."

"Was Mr. Dane standing up when you left him?"

"No. He sat down in his chair, soon as he got the drink fixed."

"Why was he washing the glass?"

"To get it clean, I reckon," the boy said pertly. "You see," he went on, catching a frigid gleam in the detective's eye, "Mr. Dane never drinks anything, during a performance. Not till he's through for the night. That's another thing he always told me. I guess he washed the glass out because it hadn't been used since yesterday and what with the heel of last night's drinks, and dust blowing in . . ."

"That will be all for now, young fellow," the detective interrupted. "Inspector Duveen will want to see you a little later, when he gets here. Until then, keep your mouth shut; if you don't, I'll put you where you won't have anybody to talk to. Understand?" He flashed his metal badge.

The boy glanced at the door of the dressing room; he could not, from where he stood, see inside.

"Has anything happened to Mr. Dane?" he asked, staring.

"Yes, he's sick!" the detective replied. "That's under your hat, too! Now beat it!"

"Right, sir." The boy went down the iron stairs.

The detective rejoined Steve and Dr. Badouine.

"Do you notice," Steve asked, "a strong smell of whiskey?"

The plainclothes man sniffed, glancing about the small, ill-ventilated room.

"No more'n I'd expect," he said, "with the window shut, and a glass that's just been used, on the table." He crossed the room, stared through the grimy panes into the alley. "Shut, but not fastened; nothing in that, though; there's bars outside."

Steve had noticed the rusty bars beyond the window. A usual protection against sneak thieves, but ample proof that no one, except the call boy could have entered the room. But was it? After the boy had left, some other visitor might have come in, joined Dane, from the corridor. He had been drinking his highball, the boy asserted, as the door was closed, but might there not have been a second drink? Steve glanced at the bottle of soda. Very little of it had been consumed; no more, he felt sure, than would have been needed for the first one. A comparatively simple test should tell. He explained his theory to the Headquarters man, who was sufficiently impressed to tear a shred of paper from the gummed flap of an envelope and paste it on the neck of the bottle.

"That will show how much was poured out," he said, "but I guess the Chief will have his own ideas. Hear him coming up now."

Voices and a creaking of heavy feet on the iron stairway announced Inspector Duveen's arrival. He stood at the door taking in the scene with hard, critical eyes. For a long, speculative moment they rested on Steve.

"Well, well, young fellow," he said ironically. "In at the death again, eh? You sure have got a fine nose for corpses."

Steve colored slightly, remembering that he had been the first to discover Mrs. Kirby's body, as well. He was about to reply, when a commotion in the corridor outside the dressing room caused him to turn.

The stage manager, aware of the growing excitement had come up to investigate, followed by several members of the cast. Duveen made short work of them.

"Mr. Dane is dead," he announced. "Heart attack. That's all I care to give out, so far. No, you needn't send for a doctor; we have one here. Go on with your show. Get the final curtain down. Let the audience leave. Everybody back stage is to stay until I'm through with them. That clear?"

"Perfectly, perfectly," the manager agreed, herding the group of actors and stage hands down the stairs. "Quiet, you people, it's the police."

Duveen turned to the doctor and Steve.

"Too bad you didn't have a chance to try any of that psychological stuff," he said with an ironic laugh.

"Unfortunately," Dr. Badouine retorted, flushing a little, "Mr. Dane was dead when we arrived. Which convinces me that Mr. Ransom and I were quite right in thinking he knew something about Mrs. Kirby's murder."

"Maybe, maybe," the Inspector said. "Well, let's have your stories—and make them snappy. After that I won't need you any more tonight."

XVII

Breakfast at Halfway House, since Mrs. Kirby's death, had been an affair of individual trays. Steve, dressing, regretted the fact; he had looked forward to a talk with Ann Vickery about Dane's sudden death. For some reason he kept thinking of it as murder.

A hunch, he had said to Dr. Badouine the night before, as they stood discussing the matter outside the theatre. But the doctor's cool, scientific brain held no place for hunches.

"I'm afraid you were right, Mr. Ransom," he had said, "in linking Dane with Mrs. Kirby's murder. Offhand, I should be inclined to say he killed her and took his own life to avoid being arrested for the crime."

"Looks like it," Steve agreed. "Although it might be just as reasonable to argue that he knew who the murderer was, and got bumped off as a result. You remember I always claimed he either stole that snapshot himself, or knew who did steal it."

"I haven't forgotten." The doctor's eyes twinkled shrewdly. "No doubt you realize the direction in which such a course of reasoning will almost certainly lead. If Dane tried to sell his knowledge to Senator Kirby . . ." for a moment the doctor paused. "Both as Mrs. Kirby's physician and her friend, I have been familiar for some time with the conditions existing between herself and her husband. The ancient domestic triangle, as old as the Garden of Eden. The French are right. We can never safely disregard their well-known maxim, *'Cherchez la femme.'*"

"Exactly," Steve said, remembering his talk with Mrs. Conover. "And the woman in the case was one of the guests at de Zara's party. Her name is Mitchell."

"So you've found that out, have you?" Dr. Badouine smiled cynically. "I could have told you about her before, had I felt at liberty to do so. My information came from Mrs. Kirby; she knew about the woman, of course. In fact, it was one of the major causes of her recent mental disturbance. Did you also notice that she, Mrs. Mitchell, was one of a party with Mr. Reed, in a box at the show tonight?"

"The devil she was!" Steve exclaimed. "I don't know the woman by sight. Look here, do you think that she and Senator Kirby . . . ?"

The doctor held up his hand.

"Please. I suggest nothing of the sort. My opinion, as I have already told you, is that Dane committed suicide. A mere guess, of course, based on conditions as we found them. To go further, pending an examination of the body, the two bottles, the glass, would be a waste of time. For all we know, the man may have died from a heart attack of some sort . . . an acute dilitation, perhaps, brought on by excessive use of alcohol. I am sorry we did not have a chance to talk with him, as I think we might have discovered something of value. Well, good night." The doctor stepped into his car.

That had been the extent of their conversation. Steve ate his breakfast, wondering what Inspector Duveen would have to report. He had just finished his coffee when a tap sounded on the bedroom door, followed at once by the sudden appearance of Parsons, the shifty-eyed and shrill-voiced second man.

"Senator Kirby would like to see you at once, sir," he said, gathering up the breakfast dishes. "In his study, please."

"Very well," Steve replied, and went down the stairs. The Senator, hunched over his desk, seemed not to have moved since the afternoon before; his large-boned face, however, was not quite so mummy-like; his cheeks showed a little more color.

"Good morning!" he said, without cordiality.

"Good morning, sir. You asked to see me?" Steve stood waiting.

"Yes. Now that the mystery of my wife's death seems explained, you will doubtless be leaving us. As soon as Inspector Duveen gets here . . ."

"Explained?" Steve asked, surprised.

"Certainly. There was never any great mystery about it, in spite of the stupidity of the police. Here!" Senator Kirby tossed a morning paper across the desk. "Sit down. And read this. I will talk to you further, when the Inspector arrives."

Steve took a chair by the window, glanced at the two-column head. "Actor Takes Life in Theatre!" "Suicide of Well-Known Leading Man!" "It is believed that the death of Lawrence Dane, prominent member of a local stock company, was the direct result of a dose of poison, self-administered in his dressing room, at an early hour last evening . . ."

On and on. Columns of it, embellished with photographs, diagrams and other "art work," sprinkled with cautious libel-avoiding phrases, such as "we are informed," or "the police think," but not, Steve noticed, containing one line or word to connect Lawrence Dane's death with the murder of Mrs. Kirby. Someone must have used influence, powerful influence, to accomplish that. Unless, of course, Inspector Duveen was merely playing safe, pending the outcome of his night's work? But why had Kirby said the case was solved?

The arrival of the Inspector himself put an end to such speculations; he seemed both tired, and out of sorts. Nor did the Senator's manner, rude to the point of hostility, improve his temper.

"I should like to know," Kirby said, "the full details regarding this fellow Dane's death."

Duveen flushed under his tan.

"I am not in the habit, Senator Kirby," he said, "of discussing the work of my department with outsiders." His eyes, very blue and steady in spite of his fatigue, flicked momentarily toward Steve.

If the Senator noticed it he concealed the fact. Frowning, he stared across the desk.

"Sit down, Inspector," he said, keying his voice as usual to an imaginary microphone, "and listen to me. I want Mr. Ransom, as well, to hear what I have to say, since he has shown such unwarranted interest in my affairs. Mrs. Kirby was brutally murdered, in my opinion, by this fellow Dane. It should have been your opinion as well, if you had shown proper intelligence in handling the case. However, that is not my purpose in calling you here. If Dane killed my wife, he is dead, and that's the end of it. No good can be served by dragging Mrs. Kirby's name into the case. On the contrary, it will cause much harm. Both to myself and to my daughter. It is the duty of the police to punish the guilty, not the innocent. Certainly it is no part of their work, to serve a venal, sensation-loving press!" Senator Kirby raised his hand in a gesture not unknown to an admiring public. "Inspector Duveen," he went on, "and this applies to you as well, young man, if this actor, Dane, *did* kill himself, if the evidence points to suicide, I want the matter to rest there. His reasons, his fear of being charged with the murder of Mrs. Kirby, must not be brought out! Now tell me the facts!"

Inspector Duveen crooked his lone trigger-finger; it was a characteristic gesture whenever he was powerfully disturbed.

"Before I answer you, Senator," he said, "tell me why you feel so sure Dane murdered your wife?"

"Because he wrote me two letters. Sly, very polite letters, saying he wanted to see me. About a certain proposition. A financial proposition, in which I could not fail to be interested."

"You have those letters?"

"No. I decided the fellow was trying to blackmail me and threw them into the fire!"

The Inspector sighed. He seemed dejected.

"Is that all?" he asked. Senator Kirby, however, refused to be drawn; he countered with another question.

"Why ask me?" he said sharply. "You know what case you had against him. Did he commit suicide or did he not? We gain nothing by arguing."

Duveen stopped crooking his finger; his mind seemed made up.

"Lawrence Dane," he announced, "was found in his dressing room, dead. From a dose of aconitine. It is the swiftest and deadliest poison known. There was none, in the whiskey bottle. None, in the soda. Traces, strong traces, were found in the bottom of his glass. The call boy who brought him the soda swears Dane had begun to drink the highball when he . . . the boy . . . went out, closed the door. Aconitine acts so quickly that if anyone else had gone into the room after the boy left, they would have found Dane either dying, or dead."

"But suppose," Steve interrupted, "there wasn't any poison in the first drink, and somebody came in and doctored a second one?"

"No." The Inspector shook his head. Mournfully. "There wasn't any second drink. Only enough soda had been poured out to fix one. We've checked that. As for fingerprints, some smudges on the whiskey bottle; Dane's clearer, on the glass. The call boy's on the soda . . . under Dane's. Also the fellow's across the street who sold the bottle. No others."

"It's quite evident what happened?" Senator Kirby growled. "Suicide!"

"I can't figure it but one way, either," Duveen said. "Dane must have put that poison in the glass himself. Either when he was over at the basin, washing it, or after the call boy left the room."

The Senator nodded. His ill-nature had largely disappeared.

"I am glad, Inspector," he announced, "to see that you have reached so sensible and logical a conclusion. Let the newspapers, the public, suppose that Dane committed suicide because of an unhappy love affair. Let them suppose what they please. But do not destroy my usefulness as a public servant, blacken my dead wife's name, and ruin my daughter's future, her social career, by publishing to the world . . ."

"I'm not in the publishing business, Senator," Duveen interrupted dryly. "If Dane hadn't killed himself I'd have arrested him this morning for the murder of your wife. Long as I can't do that now, the evidence I had against him stays in the Department's files."

"Thank you, Inspector! I won't forget it!" The Senator got up, was about to put out his hand. Duveen went on speaking.

"But if I find that Dane did *not* kill himself," he continued, "or the evidence I've got points to somebody else, I'm going to act on it, and you, or the President himself won't stop me. That is, as long as I'm head of the Detective Bureau, anyway! Don't forget the newspapers will be hammering me for a solution of your wife's murder and sooner or later I've got to give them one!" He nodded to Steve. "I can't be responsible for what Mr. Ransom may say, or do; if he has any information about Dane, or your wife, it didn't come from me."

Steve stepped forward, his lips tightening.

"Whatever I know, Senator Kirby," he said, "I shall certainly not give it to the newspapers. Nor to anyone, except Inspector Duveen. If I've tried to discover who committed the murder, it's only because I was dragged, quite accidentally, into the case. Under the circumstances, I'd better leave the house!"

"You are at liberty to stay, Mr. Ransom," the Senator put in hastily, "as long as you wish. I know you to be a gentleman, and . . ."

"Only till after the inquest this afternoon." Duveen gave Steve a small, unnoticed wink. "And all he'll have to say then will be what he found, when he walked into that room the other night. Witnesses at inquests give facts, not opinions; I'm sure Mr. Ransom can be trusted to keep his to himself."

Senator Kirby nodded. Steve and the Inspector went out.

At the front door they paused. Duveen was grinning, not mirthfully.

"Damned old hypocrite!" he muttered under his breath.

"Going in town?" Steve asked.

"Yep. A little office work. Why?"

"I've got an idea. Need your help to carry it out. Also, I want to take Miss Vickery along to lunch. So I thought if you had your car, we'd drive in with you; I'll bring her back in a cab."

"What's this idea you're talking about?"

"I want to stop at Dane's room, in the Piedmont for a minute. I know your men will be on the job there, and without your authority wouldn't let me in. So if you don't mind fixing it . . ."

"Still trying to help us poor dicks out, are you?" the Inspector grumbled, but there was humor in his eye. "All right, young fellow . . . get your girl; that will make it easier for me to keep an eye on both of you."

"Thanks," Steve said, and went in search of Ann. He found her in the garden, gathering narcissus. She was, he thought, even more fresh and lovely than the pale, unusual flowers.

"Good morning, Little Red Riding Hood," she grinned.

"Morning, beautiful!" Steve squeezed her fingers.

"Still looking for that kiss?"

"And that corner. It's a long road, you know, that hasn't one or two. Get your hat; we're going to do a little high-class sleuthing."

Ann ran up the stairs, came down again, wearing the bunch of flowers at her waist. The Inspector, noticing her eagerness, chuckled.

"Anyway, Miss Vickery," he said, "you're going to give the newsreel boys and camera men a thrill; there's a mob of them just outside."

They ran the gantlet of clicking cameras, the Inspector growling his stereotyped "Nothing new." In the police car he became more communicative.

"Keen as buzzards!" he exclaimed, giving Steve a broad wink. "Must be some kind of a sixth sense, the way those birds can smell scandal a mile off; I don't wonder the old boy is feeling jumpy."

"You've heard of a certain Mrs. Mitchell, I suppose?" Steve asked. "Known as 'Babs?'"

Duveen tried to assume his poker face, gave it up under the influence of Steve's smile.

"Maybe," he growled. "Why?"

"Did you know she was in a box at the theatre last night? With Luke Reed?"

"How did you know it?"

"Dr. Badouine and I stood back for a while, watching the finish of the second act."

"So what?"

"Nothing . . . yet. But being in show business myself, and at least able to find my way about a theatre, I can't help thinking how easy it is to get back stage from a box. Especially a box that happens to be right alongside the connecting door from the front of the house, which this one was. It may not mean anything, but then again, it might."

"How? Dane, according to the evidence, was alone when he took that drink, soon as he got to his room, at ten-twenty—"

"Ten-nineteen, to be exact, when he left the stage," Steve interrupted. "I timed it."

"Well?"

"Well, Dr. Badouine and I showed up seven or eight minutes later; I didn't time that, but I stopped to smoke a cigarette. Thought we'd give Dane a chance to get his make-up off. If he sent the call boy for the soda as soon as he left the stage, he could have had it in two minutes . . . three at the outside; you remember he told the boy to hurry. Allow another minute for opening the bottle, mixing the drink, that makes four, and gives us an interval of four or five minutes, during which a lot of people might have gone into his dressing room."

"And found him dead," the Inspector grunted, not much interested. "So what?"

Steve continued to smile. Hopefully.

"That's where my idea comes in," he said. "It's probably a dud, but I'd like to find out. If it doesn't work, there's no harm done and I can probably use the thing in my next detective play."

"I hope you don't put me in it." Ann laughed. "Look what happened, the last time you mixed me up in one of your interesting plots."

"May be the best thing that ever happened to you, angel," Steve grinned at her, lighting a cigarette. "To either of us. I'm hoping, before the show is over, to make you see it that way."

Duveen was scowling; there was no humor in his cool blue eyes.

"What are you getting at, young fellow?" he snapped. "Spill it."

"Well, to start with, you say you knew Senator Kirby's lady friend, Mrs. Mitchell, was in a box at the theatre with Luke Reed last night?"

"Sure I knew it. Same as I knew you and Dr. Badouine were there. What do you think I've been doing, taking a rest cure? Come again."

"All right. Here's another one. Did you know Mrs. Mitchell was among those present at de Zara's studio party, the night that photograph was snitched?"

This time the Inspector's dead-pan mask went completely to pieces; he had been up the better part of two nights and had lost a great deal of sleep.

"The hell she was!" he muttered. "I had that party checked . . . didn't get her name."

"I guess she wasn't using it, on the Senator's account. Posed as a friend of Luke Reed's. What's more, she showed a particular interest in de Zara's gold-inlaid souvenir box. Wanted to buy it, I understand. That gave her an excuse to examine the thing. Possibly, to steal the photograph."

"How did you find this out?" Duveen seemed hugely annoyed.

"Just luck," Steve said. "Gossip. The female of the species, you know, very deadly." He was thinking of Mrs. Conover. "You might try what I've just told you on your adding machine . . . along with the fact that girls will be girls, and some of them, if they can't get a man one way might try another, even blackmail . . . murder . . . to

remove an obstacle from the road to happiness. You know
. . . everything for love . . . and a fat bank account."

Duveen frowned, shaking his head.

"If you mean Mrs. Mitchell might have murdered Mrs.
Kirby," he said, "I've been all over that. So far, no pota-
toes. Dane was my man. I think he stole the picture himself. We know he wrote a letter to Mrs. Kirby that somebody burned . . . tried to at least."

"You don't think it possible, then, that the Mitchell
woman stole the picture, that Dane saw her do it and was
killed before he could spill the beans?"

"Certainly it's possible she took the picture out of that
box. But she didn't murder Dane. Nobody did. He killed
himself. The evidence proves it, beyond any question."

"I know it does," Steve said, as the car drew up in front
of the Piedmont Hotel. "No need of your going up to the
room with me, Inspector, unless you want to. Just tip off
one of your dicks; I shan't be a minute."

Duveen crooked his finger at a plainclothes man loung-
ing near the hotel door.

"This is Mr. Ransom, Len," he said. "Take him to
Dane's room. The boys got anything up there yet?"

"Not a thing, Chief, Ryan tells me, except a bunch of
unpaid bills, and a flock of empty bottles in the clothes'
closet."

Steve got out of the car.

"If it's all the same to you, Inspector," he said, "I'll
bring back a couple of those empties."

"Go as far as you like," Duveen remarked sourly. "But
if you're thinking about fingerprints, you're wasting your
time."

Ann lit a cigarette, sat staring at the smoke from it. She
was thinking that the spring sunshine was very warm and
pleasant, and contemplating the curious design of life,
which made use of death, of murder, to bring two people

like Steve and herself together, ready to start another series of whorls in the intricate and ever-changing pattern. At least she felt ready. As for Steve . . .

He came back carrying a package wrapped in newspaper under his arm.

"All set," he said, climbing into the car.

"What do you expect to do with bottles?" The Inspector was smiling, but there was a cold, professional gleam in his eye.

"Wouldn't want me to give away the show in advance, would you?" Steve grinned. "Especially as I'm not at all sure there's going to be any show. Ten to one my little experiment won't work. When we get to your office . . ."

"May I come?" Ann asked.

"Of course, if the Inspector doesn't object. It always helps, to have an appreciative audience."

Duveen nodded. When they reached Police Headquarters he brushed a maze of questions, of messages aside, went to his private office.

"Get going, young fellow!" he said sharply. "And make it snappy, I've got work to do!" He waved to chairs, sat down.

Steve unwrapped his package, placed the two empty bottles on the Inspector's desk. Ann, watching his hands, saw that they were shaking.

"You found a pocket knife on Dane's body, didn't you?" he asked, eagerly.

"Not on his body . . . the make-up shelf. With his money and keys."

"I'll want that. And the bottle of Scotch he took his last drink from."

The Inspector spoke into a desk telephone. Steve was staring at the two empty bottles.

"Dane always drank White Label," he said to Ann.

"I'll have those things here in a couple of minutes." Duveen swung around in his swivel chair. "Maybe I'm thick, but I don't just see what you're driving at."

"Well," Steve said, "it's merely an idea. I can't say, yet, whether it will work. But you admit, don't you, that Dane was drinking the poisoned liquor when the call boy left him . . . five or six minutes before Dr. Badouine and I arrived on the scene?"

"Sure. And from what the Medical Examiner tells me, about the effects of aconitine, he was probably dead by the time the boy reached the foot of the stairs."

"Exactly. So of course it would have been easy enough for anybody to have gone into his dressing room, during that five or six minutes, after the call boy left? Anybody sitting in a box, for instance, very close to the door leading back stage."

"What for? It doesn't make sense. Dane was already dead."

"I know. But just the same, let me put off telling you my ideas about that until I see how my little experiment works out." Steve turned as a young man came into the room; he carried a nearly-filled bottle of whiskey in one hand, a silver pocket knife at the end of a keychain, in the other.

"This stuff has been gone over, Chief," he said, placing the bottle, the knife, on Duveen's desk. "You've seen the report."

"Thanks, Marty." The Inspector watched the young man go out. "Well?" he went on impatiently, when the door had closed. "I'm waiting."

Steve took up the knife, pulled out the small corkscrew hinged to the back of it.

"Dane always carried this," he said. "A relic of pre-prohibition days." He took up one of the bottles he had brought from the hotel, inserted the sharp point of the corkscrew into the hole which showed at the top of the cork. "You'll notice," he went on, turning the knife slowly around, "that it goes right in. Easily. No effort required . . ."

"Why wouldn't it?" the Inspector grumbled. "Nothing surprising about that, the hole's already there."

"Exactly." Steve had withdrawn the corkscrew from the first bottle, was repeating his experiment with the second. "That's just the point. Fits this one, too. Now, Inspector, try it on the bottle found in Dane's dressing room." He handed the knife to Duveen. "If I'm right in my guess as to what happened, you'll score a miss."

Using his left hand, the Inspector threaded the point of the corkscrew into the tiny hole at the top of the cork, turned the knife around, as Steve had done a moment before. Nothing happened; the screw refused to advance.

"Don't force it!" Steve cautioned, touching Duveen's arm. "Looks as if I was right! Wait a minute!" He took a penknife from his pocket, removed the cork from one of the empty bottles, sliced it cleanly down the middle. "There! You see?" He held the half of the cork under Inspector Duveen's eyes. A series of small, dark openings, staggered alternately right and left made a pattern on the smooth cut face of it. "Notice how close together the holes are? That's because Dane's pocket corkscrew hasn't much distance between its turns . . . much pitch! Now cut the other cork in half . . . the one from the bottle found in his dressing room!" Steve watched the Inspector eagerly as he sliced the second cork in two. "Look at that! The holes are a lot further apart! Which shows the bottle wasn't opened with Dane's corkscrew! Yet there it was, right on the make-up shelf at his elbow! Why didn't he use it?"

"Why?" Ann whispered, breathless.

"Because," Steve said quickly, "he didn't open the bottle."

Inspector Duveen, sitting very straight in his chair, crashed an incomplete fist on the desk-top.

"By God and little fishes, Son!" he shouted. "You've got it! They switched bottles on us! After he was dead!"

"Right!" Steve was grinning. "Somebody must have gone into Dane's dressing room during the second act, while he was on stage, and poisoned his whiskey! And then, after he'd passed out from drinking a slug of it, they came back to the room, took away the poisoned bottle and left a good one, this one, in its place. To make his death look like suicide! When all the time . . ."

"When all the time," Duveen interrupted harshly, "he'd been bumped off . . . murdered! Probably by the same smart guy that did for Mrs. Kirby!" For a moment the Inspector sat glowering at the whiskey bottles in front of him. Suddenly he put out his hand. "Mr. Ransom," he said. "I'm obliged to you. That was nice work!"

"Just a lucky hunch," Steve grinned. "I sometimes have them." He glanced at Ann.

XVIII

Ann Vickery leaned forward in her chair; the sudden turn of events had left her a bit confused.

"I don't quite see . . ." she began.

"It's like this, miss." The Inspector ticked off the points on the fingers of his good hand. "No poison found in the whiskey bottle! None, in the soda! Aconitine, very deadly, in a glass that had just been washed clean! Suicide, of course! No other conclusion possible, since nobody could have put the poison in his glass but himself! Well, he did put it there, without knowing it! Only the bottle he poured it from was later taken away, and another, quite harmless, left in its place! Clever, all right, damned clever!"

"But when?"

"During the four or five minutes between the time he was murdered, and the discovery of the body by Dr. Badouine and Mr. Ransom."

"You'd think," Ann objected, "that whoever did it would have been seen carrying the good bottle in, taking the poisoned one away."

"They aren't quarts." Steve waved toward the desk. "Fifth. Smaller! Look!" He snatched up one of the slender bottles, slipped it into his trousers pocket. "Easy enough. Only the neck shows. And that would be covered by a coat.

Especially a woman's coat. I'll bet right now a woman went into that dressing room during the evening . . ."

Duveen was juggling the bits of cut cork. "What gave you the idea?" he said.

"Something you told Senator Kirby this morning," Steve replied. "You said you didn't get clear prints of Dane's fingers, on the whiskey bottle, although you did, on the glass and the bottle of soda."

"Right," the Inspector nodded. "The way I figured it, his fingers slipped a little when he put down the bottle . . . blurred the prints. Likely to happen, when you don't get a firm grip . . . and I knew Dane's hands would have cold cream on them. I ought to have paid more attention to those smudges," he added morosely.

"I got to thinking it over," Steve went on, "and the idea came into my head that maybe the bottle had been handled with gloves. If so . . . why? Perhaps I'm just naturally curious. Also I remembered seeing Dane open a bottle of Scotch with that pocket corkscrew of his, when I was in his room at the hotel. So I figured that if the bottles *had* been switched the corks ought to show it, since the bottle brought in to replace the poisoned one would have had to be opened in advance . . . some of the whiskey poured out. Dane, you remember, wasn't drinking from a full bottle. The murderer probably dumped the excess whiskey into the wash-basin. I noticed a strong smell of alcohol in the room . . . spoke to your man about it, Inspector, at the time. The only mistake our killer made was not thinking of the cork."

"The best of them slip up somewhere," Duveen growled. "I suppose, because Dane knew too much, he had to be got rid of in a hurry. That half-charred note to Mrs. Kirby we found in the fireplace was probably about the Cannes photograph. Had just a couple of legible words, and his signature on it. I figured Dane had been there, quarreled

with her over the amount he was to get, killed her. Thrown
the card in the fire. He'd have been arrested, this morning,
if the murderer hadn't got ahead of me, last night. Now
I've got to start all over again."

"If we knew who stole that picture from de Zara's apartment . . ." Steve began.

"Wouldn't prove anything." Duveen said irritably.
"Whoever took the snapshot could have turned it over to
somebody else. Somebody like Senator Kirby," he added,
frowning. "Far as that goes, we don't even know it was
taken, the night of the party. The lock of that box could
have been picked any time, by a smart crook. Haven't any
proof, in fact, it was stolen at all; that's the Count's story
but how do we know he isn't lying? Pretty neat, if he carried that photograph to Mrs. Kirby's house himself. The
maid, Georgette, gives him an alibi, but she hasn't said
anything, so far, about Miss Kirby being there with the
two of them, on the night of the murder."

"There are the pearls," Steve suggested.

"Don't mean a thing! That phony set may have been
planted, or Mrs. Kirby may have had them on when the
murderer choked her. No way to tell which. Same with
the hairs she had in her fingers. They show she grabbed
at somebody wearing a wig, but whether it was a man or a
woman, light or dark, we haven't any idea. Same way with
the rest of the clues. The pen-holder proves nothing . . .
it was wiped clean. We don't know why that china plaque
that hid the wall safe was swung open, or who opened it.
Even the papers that were torn, burned, don't prove who
burned them, or why. Or how those figures of yours, Mr.
Ransom, happened to be destroyed along with the rest.
Unless you're guilty, it doesn't make sense."

"No," Steve said. "It doesn't. I've been wondering about
that call boy. What was he doing, during those five or six
minutes?"

"Chinning with one of the stage hands," Duveen replied. "I've been into all that. Says he was, at any rate, and the other guy backs him up. Except he isn't exactly sure about the time."

"Well, here's one thing that might have happened. Say somebody . . . some woman . . . went to Dane's dressing room during the second act and poisoned his whiskey. Carried the aconitine in a small vial in her purse. No need for her to come back; the call boy, or anybody else . . . even some member of the company . . . might have been bribed to slip into Dane's room with a good bottle of whiskey . . . take away the poisoned one . . ."

Duveen threw up his hands.

"Hell and high water!" he exclaimed. "Anything is possible in this case! It's cockeyed! I've been over the evidence a hundred times and I can't get the answer."

"Maybe Senator Kirby can supply it," Steve said.

"Maybe! Or Luke Reed! Or this Mitchell dame! Looks bad for all three of them. Plenty of motive! Plenty of money! No satisfactory alibi . . . at least not yet. But when it comes to accusing United States senators of little things like murder you've got to watch your step . . . can't go at them with a piece of rubber hose!" One of the telephone instruments on the desk began to ring furiously. Duveen picked it up. "You folks run along," he said. "I've got a lot to do, now. Thanks for your help, Mr. Ransom; don't forget the inquest's at three-thirty."

Ann was very quiet all the way to the street.

"Just time," Steve said, looking at his watch, "to take a look at the cherry blossoms before we have lunch." He waved to a cab. "How about it, sweetness?"

"Fine," Ann nodded, and resumed her thinking. Ten minutes later she asked a question.

"At what time," she said slowly, "do you suppose this mysterious woman went to Mr. Dane's dressing room and poisoned his whiskey?"

"During the second act, I figure. While he was on stage. Around nine-thirty, say. Why?"

"Soon after we finished dinner last night."

"Skip it, honey!" Steve exclaimed. "I can swear you never went near the theatre, if that's what is on your mind."

"It's only a few blocks from the hotel."

"So what?"

"The woman with de Zara! And he had a bottle under his arm . . ."

"Good God!" Steve muttered. "Why didn't you say that to the Inspector? It's a natural . . ."

"Better to wait." Ann's eyes were very tender. "You see, there's Jean."

XIX

Inspector Duveen rang the bell of the house on Connecticut Avenue, asked to see Judge Tyson.

The old gentleman maintained no law office in Washington; his home was on the Eastern Shore of Maryland. When the affairs of a few special clients required his presence in the city he stopped at the home of a married niece.

The Inspector, waiting in the smartly-appointed drawing room, was far from sure the Judge would see him. As Mrs. Kirby's personal counsel he might well decide to stand on his rights and refuse to be questioned. Still, there was a chance.

To Duveen's surprise the old gentleman appeared at once, beaming like an amiable and benevolent cherub.

"Good morning, Duveen," he said. "Sit down. And tell me what I can do for you."

The Inspector sank into a chair, not hopeful. Experience had taught him that such outward geniality was apt to prove more impenetrable than other and less subtle forms of armor.

"You've read of Lawrence Dane's death, no doubt?" he began.

"Yes." The Judge raised his eyebrow. "Suicide, I understand."

"No," Duveen said. "Murder." He spoke almost carelessly, watching the old gentleman's face for some change of expression. None came.

"Really?" The Judge inquired, fiddling with his nose-glasses. "I can't say I'm surprised."

"Why not?"

Inspector Duveen snapped the question almost viciously.

"I imagine he knew too much."

This was precisely the turn in the conversation for which Duveen had been hoping.

"Too much about what?"

"About Mrs. Kirby's affairs. And the Senator's . . ."

"Why do you say that?"

The Judge's geniality vanished. His round, rosy face no longer suggested a cherub, amiable or otherwise.

"You realize, Inspector," he said coldly, "that I am under no obligation to answer your questions. Nor is it my habit to discuss my clients' affairs in public. If I do so now, it is solely in the interests of justice."

"Of course." Duveen nodded. "I understand."

"Very well. Upon that basis, I will explain my statement. On the day of her death Mrs. Kirby received a letter from this man Dane requesting an interview. I was at the house, attending a luncheon party. When it was over she showed me the letter. Although couched in cautious terms, it seemed to me that an invitation to blackmail could be read between the lines. Mrs. Kirby asked my advice and I told her to pay no attention to the letter, that once in the clutches of a man of that sort it would be impossible to get out. As a result, she tore the card in two . . . the note had been written on an ordinary correspondence card . . . and threw the pieces into the fire, along with some other papers."

"Yes," Duveen said. "I found one of the halves, badly charred, against the brickwork. Have you any idea what the information was that Dane proposed to sell?"

The Judge paused for a moment, considering.

"To answer your question," he said, "I am obliged to tell you something of Mrs. Kirby's domestic affairs. Her husband had for months been trying to force her to give him a divorce in order that he might marry again. She refused. I suspect this man Dane had some information regarding Senator Kirby and the woman in the case which might have been of value to Mrs. Kirby in opposing divorce proceedings . . ."

"Not about the Cannes photograph, then?"

"The Cannes photograph?" Duveen's question jarred the Judge from his smooth complacency. "You know of that?"

"Certainly. The matter has been kept from the newspapers, but we found the picture under Mrs. Kirby's head."

"Dear me!" The old gentleman put on his nose-glasses, took them off again. "This is a surprise. I thought de Zara . . ."

"Count de Zara claims the photograph was stolen from him during a party he gave at his studio not long ago. You were there."

"And so," the Judge added hastily, "was Lawrence Dane. He could have taken the picture."

"I thought that too . . . thought he had killed Mrs. Kirby . . . until I found he'd been murdered himself! Now I figure he knew who did take it."

"Just so, just so!" Judge Tyson sat with his eyes half-closed, thinking rapidly. "Is it your idea, Inspector, that I stole that photograph? On Mrs. Kirby's account? To prevent her husband from securing it . . . using it against her in divorce proceedings?"

"No." Duveen felt now that he had secured the upper hand; his opponent was on the defensive. "I make no such accusation. My hope was that having been present, you might have some idea who did!"

"Of course! I see your point. This is a great surprise to me. I wondered at the time why not only Senator Kirby, but Mrs. Mitchell and Luke Reed were at that party. No reason why the Senator shouldn't have been there; he has never opposed his daughter's marriage to de Zara. But to bring Mrs. Mitchell along! Rather bad taste, I thought, even at a bohemian affair. Now I begin to understand! If *she* got hold of the picture, think what a weapon it would have been in her hands and the Senator's!"

"Am I then to understand that Mrs. Mitchell is the woman Senator Kirby intends to marry?" the Inspector asked.

"Of course. I supposed you knew that."

"I'd heard so." Duveen smiled, frostily. "Glad to have your confirmation. What can you tell me about the lady? As Mrs. Kirby's attorney I assume you've had her looked up."

"Yes. Thoroughly. She began as a dancer, in Broadway musical shows. Married at eighteen . . . a college boy . . . divorced him in '29, when his father lost all his money. Six months later she married again—a wealthy horse own-er and racing man, Andy Mitchell. You may have heard of him. Like most gamblers he is always winning fortunes, then losing them. She divorced him during one of his losing streaks. Now she is looking for a third victim."

"Has Senator Kirby any money?"

"Oh, yes. Mines, timber, in the south-west. No such fortune as his wife possessed, but . . . ample."

"Why should he want to marry Mrs. Mitchell?"

The Judge chuckled. Grimly. He was a bachelor.

"Why should any man want to marry any woman?" he asked. "Senator Kirby is over fifty. I suppose he imagines himself in love. It isn't difficult, at his age, to develop that illusion . . . especially when in the hands of a clever woman."

"You think Mrs. Mitchell is clever, then?"

"She must be, to make a man willing to leave a wife worth twenty millions.

Clever, and unscrupulous, since she deliberately set out to break up Mrs. Kirby's home."

"Unscrupulous enough to commit murder, do you think? In order to get what she was after?"

The Judge shrugged, shaking his head.

"Other women have. I cannot speak for Mrs. Mitchell."

Duveen sat staring at his lone forefinger. He had succeeded in doing what he had come to do . . . had made the old gentleman talk.

"Has it occurred to you, Judge Tyson," he said, "that if Mrs. Mitchell did steal that photograph she may have come to Halfway House the other night, threatened to make use of it, unless Mrs. Kirby agreed to divorce her husband? We know Mrs. Kirby received a secret visitor, a woman, according to all accounts, shortly before she was killed."

"No." The Judge sat nodding his head, like a plump Chinese figurine. "Such a thought did not occur to me, since I did not know, until you told me just now, that the picture had been found at the scene of the murder. Since you say it was, I am quite prepared to believe what you suggest."

Inspector Duveen gazed at the floor. At last the picture was becoming clearer . . . the various clues were beginning to fit into place. A determined, unscrupulous woman. Glimpsing the snapshot in de Zara's souvenir box, stealing it. An ex-actress, familiar with the use of make-up, wigs. Disguising herself, not on Mrs. Kirby's account, but to avoid recognition by the servants. Mrs. Kirby, knowing in advance of the visit, providing herself with a large sum in untraceable bonds, hoping to buy the photograph, buy her visitor off. Exposing the wall safe to get at the money . . . not opening it, because her offer had been rejected. A furious quarrel between the two women . . . Mrs. Kirby choked . . . her string of pearls broken, scattered on the floor . . .

picked up, under the supposition that they were real . . .
tossed into the flower vase as soon as it was discovered
they were not! Murder, with the first weapon at hand, to
avoid subsequent accusation, disgrace! The hands of the
clock turned forward to make it strike twelve, so that if
Mrs. Kirby's voice had been overheard by anyone in the
house, she would appear to have been alive at midnight.
A quick escape, then, to join someone else . . . Senator
Kirby, perhaps, or Luke Reed, and thus establish an alibi
for that hour. Leaving the photograph behind to throw
suspicion on de Zara. Or, in her excitement, forgetting it.
A telephone message from Dane the next day, saying that
he had witnessed the theft of the picture. Ample motive,
there, for the actor's murder. Mrs. Mitchell in a box at the
theatre . . . hurrying back stage to poison his liquor . . .
learning, then, the kind of whiskey needed to replace it.
Luke Reed, perhaps, sent to buy the necessary bottle. The
two bottles switched, possibly with the connivance of the
call boy. Everything seemed to fit, the Inspector thought,
everything but Mrs. Kirby's cry about a nail. Most likely
she *had* said "blackmail."

Judge Tyson interrupted his train of thought. "Have
you questioned Mrs. Mitchell?" he asked.

"No." Duveen got up. "I wanted to talk to you first.
The information you've given me will help."

The old gentleman was once more the shrewd, cautious
lawyer, dignified, reserved.

"I have spoken rather freely," he said. "Too freely, perhaps. I ask that you do not quote me, otherwise I shall be
obliged to deny any statements you make."

Duveen nodded, took his leave, feeling, subconsciously,
that Judge Tyson had been rather anxious to throw blame
for the murder on Mrs. Mitchell. Well, perhaps that was
natural; he had been Mrs. Kirby's friend. It would be

possible to tell better, the Inspector thought, after he had talked to the woman.

The small house in Georgetown was very gay, with its peacock blue door and shutters, its flower-filled window boxes. A trim mulatto maid asked him to wait in the parlor . . . Duveen smiled at the word . . . while she took up his name.

He did not have to wait long. Mrs. Mitchell appeared almost at once, very smart in a brown afternoon frock; she wore a hat and was apparently dressed to go out.

"I've only a moment," she said, taking his hand. "On my way to lunch. I know who you are, of course. Well, any questions you'd like to ask . . ."

Duveen looked at her, surprised. Rather larger than the average . . . big boned. Like an English woman, he thought. Her handshake had been muscular, firm. A strong, hard hand, for managing horses . . . he'd heard she had ridden a good deal, after marrying Andy Mitchell. Or for gripping other women's throats! Somehow Duveen found difficulty in imagining it, in spite of his array of clues. Mrs. Mitchell seemed unusually frank and open in manner. A man's woman. Handsome, rather than pretty. Crinkly, honey-colored hair. Hazel-green eyes, large and attractive. He pulled himself together with a laugh, remembering what the Judge had said about men in the hands of clever women.

"Mrs. Mitchell," he began, "I'm not going to keep you long. Certain questions, you understand . . . a matter of routine. You were at the theatre last night, I believe?"

"Of course. With Mr. Reed. And two friends of his, a Mr. and Mrs. Green, from Richmond. Why? Is it about that man Dane's suicide?"

"In a way, yes. You knew him, I understand."

"I'd met him. Once. At Count de Zara's apartment."

"Did you see him last night?"

"Certainly. He was in the play."

"I mean personally."

"No. I should have had no reason to talk to him . . . to go back stage."

"Did you leave your box at all, during the performance?"

"Yes. At the intermissions. And once, I think, for a cigarette in the ladies' room, during the second act."

"I see. And the night before. Where did you spend the evening?"

"You mean the night Mrs. Kirby was killed, of course. I spent it here. The earlier part, at least. Later I went for a drive."

"Alone?"

"No. With Mr. Reed and . . . a friend."

"Will you give me the friend's name?"

"No. I prefer not to." The woman was quite calm and self-possessed. Duveen, meeting her eyes, knew he had learned all she meant to tell him. He dropped his gaze, gave a slight start as he noticed the pin she wore at her neck. A gold horseshoe, set with rubies. Across it, a rather curiously shaped metal bar.

"That is a very attractive bit of jewelry, Mrs. Mitchell," he said, watching her face. "That pointed bar, now?"

"It's a horseshoe nail," the woman replied indifferently. "From one of the shoes Man of War was wearing when he won the Kentucky Derby. My husband, Mr. Mitchell, cleaned up on the race, and had the pin made for me as a souvenir of the occasion; he knew the owner."

Inspector Duveen nodded, his brain going around in circles. Was the woman innocent, or cleverly acting? The horseshoe pin might be only a chance coincidence . . . he had been deceived, led astray by coincidences before. And it might be the solution of the mystery. Confused, uncertain, he went back to his office, realizing that so far as Mrs. Mitchell was concerned he had no case.

The pile of reports on his desk had grown thicker; he ran through them, but found no light. The murderer had been enormously careful to cover his tracks, leave no valuable clues.

Fingerprints? Nothing. The pen, the door of the safe, even the glazed surface of the Cannes snapshot had been wiped clean. The strands of dead hair showed a wig, but a canvass of costumers, wigmakers in both Washington and Baltimore had not traced its purchaser, nor had Duveen expected it would. Reports from the laboratory indicated that the wig was an old one; whoever had used it might have had the thing in their possession for years. Mrs. Mitchell, for instance; she had once been on the stage. By now, having served its purpose, it had probably been destroyed.

He pushed the reports aside, scowling. A sweet case. He had hoped to break it, before the Major got back, but there seemed little chance of that, now. He glanced up as one of his men came in.

"Well, Hunter?" he asked. "Anything new?"

"I been checking up on Ransom's alibi," the detective said. "Nothing doing; that waitress, Katie Bolek, isn't expected to live."

"Hm . . . m. You been to the theatre again?"

"Just now. There was a slim, dark woman called to see Lawrence Dane . . ."

"I talked to that doorkeeper last night! He didn't say anything, then, about a woman." The Inspector scowled.

"The old bozo was pretty upset. Now he tells me this dame showed up at the stage entrance around nine-thirty, soon after the second act began . . . said she was Dane's wife, and he'd told her, if he wasn't in his dressing room, to wait."

"Did Dane have a wife?"

"Search me. You know actors."

"Get a good description of her?"

"Say, Chief, that doorkeeper's so nearsighted he can't see the end of his nose. Just a doddering old wreck. He said 'tall, dark, good-looking.' That's the score. Only about fifty thousand like it, in Washington."

"When did she go out?"

"She didn't. Not by the stage entrance. Probably through the house. Nobody would have noticed her, with the lights down; probably thought she was one of the ushers."

"Or," Duveen said grimly, "she might have gone into a box."

"Sure she might. Anyway, it wasn't that red-headed French maid; she's locked up. What about Miss Kirby?"

"In her room all evening, according to reports."

"How about the Vickery girl?"

"Having dinner with Ransom, at the Willard; he brought her home in his car at 9.45."

Hunter scratched his ear, frowning.

"I don't like to butt in Chief," he said, "but what time did they leave the hotel?"

"About fifteen minutes past nine. Rafferty didn't have orders to tail them home."

"Then they could of stopped at the theatre, on the way. Must have stopped somewhere; it wouldn't take them half an hour to drive out to the Senator's house."

"They could have ridden around. Nothing in that, Hunter . . . those two are in love . . ."

"Maybe. But I can't get it out of my noodle, Chief, that they were there on the ground when the old lady was bumped off. All we know about what happened is what they tell us."

"Nonsense!" Duveen shook his head. "Strangers. Never met before, except at lunch."

"What of it? Say this Ransom gets to the house that night a few minutes earlier than he claims he did. Say he looks through the window, sees the girl, and Mrs. Kirby, dead. He goes in . . . Miss Vickery works on his sympathies, tells him she has a fortune in pearls tucked away in that vase . . . which goes back to the conservatory first thing in the morning. She wouldn't know the pearls were phony, then. How do we know he didn't fall for it? Fall for her? We've both seen cases. A guy would have to be plenty tough, Chief, to turn a swell piece of dress goods like that up, on a murder charge. A lot of 'em go soft, when a dame in trouble appeals to their better natures, switches on the waterworks."

"What about the photograph?" Duveen growled. "You said yourself whoever left it there figured to frame de Zara. Maybe that was the girl's idea, too."

"Hell! Where would she get it?"

"If Dane sent that picture to Mrs. Kirby, or gave it to her, earlier in the day, it might have been there in one of the desk drawers."

Inspector Duveen tapped the edge of his desk with a lead pencil.

"Hunter," he said, "I think you're all wrong. But maybe I am. Mrs. Kirby was murdered around a quarter to twelve, according to Miss Vickery's story. Ransome claims he didn't reach the house until nine or ten minutes later. You see if you can dig up anybody who saw him drive into the side lane. Saw his car. If he's lying, we'll know something. Personally, while I like the young fellow, if we could pin this murder on him and the girl it would take a great load off my mind."

"I get you, Chief," Hunter said. "There's always the political angle."

"Pin it on them honestly, I mean. I'm not looking to frame anybody. Now get going."

"Right." Hunter paused at the door. "I forgot to say Mr. Luke Reed is waiting to see you. Fit to be hogtied."

"Tell them to send him in," Duveen sighed.

Mr. Reed came into the office, raging.

"What's the idea, Duveen?" he snarled angrily.

"I want to see you." The Inspector waved to a chair. "Sit down. There are a couple of questions . . ."

"Such as . . . ?"

"Such as where were you the night Mrs. Kirby was murdered? Say from ten till twelve?"

"Driving in my car."

"Anybody with you?"

"Yes."

"Who?"

"Senator Kirby."

"He doesn't say so."

"You mean he hasn't, so far. He will, at the inquest today."

"Fixed it up with him, have you?"

"You know that's a lie, Duveen. The Senator will testify he was in my car that night from ten to twelve. I shall do the same . . ."

"Where did you drive?"

"Nowhere in particular; we wanted the air."

"Alone?"

"No. There was a lady with us."

"Who?"

"I prefer not to say."

"You don't have to, Reed." The Inspector was crooking his trigger finger. "I've already talked to her."

"I know you have." The lawyer's fox-like face drew into a scowl. "However, it will not be necessary to drag her into the matter. Senator Kirby's word, and mine, will be quite enough to establish an alibi."

"But not enough," Duveen said slowly, "to prove that Mrs. Mitchell wasn't at the Senator's house."

Reed's lips, rather thin, curled back to show rodentlike teeth.

"Inspector Duveen!" he said, "don't you think you would be wiser to spend your time tracking down reasonable suspects, such as this man de Zara, or the young fellow, Ransom, who discovered the body? I don't believe his story. As for de Zara, he had more to gain from Mrs. Kirby's death than anyone else."

"I'm not overlooking them," Duveen growled. "Mrs. Mitchell stood to gain a lot, too. A chance to marry Senator Kirby."

"Have you the slightest possible evidence to connect her with the murder?" Reed asked, striving to control his temper.

"Not yet. I'm looking for it. She was in a box with you at the theatre last night."

"What of it?"

"Nothing . . . if she didn't go back stage."

"Go back stage? I don't get you." Mr. Reed seemed genuinely bewildered.

"Are you ready to swear she didn't leave that box during the second act?"

"I am."

"She told me she went to the ladies' room . . . smoked a cigarette."

Luke Reed sprang to his feet; his voice was acid enough to burn the varnish from Duveen's desk.

"Look here!" he cried. "You lay off my friends or by the living God I'll break you!"

Inspector Duveen raised his mangled hand; his eyes were shreds of blue ice.

"See that, Mr. Reed?" he asked, crooking his lone fore-finger over the stumps. "I didn't get it running away from a fight! Don't try to give me orders; nobody does that, but Major Bliss!"

"You blithering fool!" Mr. Reed's face was scarlet. "You can't drag Senator Kirby into this mess! He's too big a man . . . too important! It will hurt his political friends . . . hurt the party! We can't have his personal affairs smeared all over the front pages, just because a dumb detective . . ."

The Inspector rose from his chair, towering almost a foot above the undersized lawyer.

"I told the Senator this morning," he said, "that I wasn't giving anything to the newspapers I could keep out. When I said that, I didn't know this actor, Dane, had been mur-dered!"

"Murdered?" The lawyer's face was a sheet of grey paper.

"That's what I said . . . murdered!"

Duveen was shaking with rage. "I'm not here in the Department to play politics! My job is to work against crime. Maybe I'm dumb at it, but if so, that's my hard luck. If you don't like the way I'm running this office, see Major Bliss! He'll be back in town tomorrow. When he says lay off, which he won't, I'll listen to it! Not before! In the meanwhile, if you come in here again telling me what I ought to do, I'll throw you out on your ear! Get me?"

"Get you?" Mr. Reed was livid. "By Heaven, I *will* get you, Duveen, if it's the last thing I ever do!" He rushed from the office.

Duveen sank back into his chair. A quotation, remin-iscent of high school days, drifted through his brain. A Shakespearean quotation, having to do with one who, guilty, did protest too much.

"This," the Inspector sighed, "is one hell of a case! But I've got to go through with it!"

XX

To both Steve and Ann, the inquest into Mrs. Kirby's death proved less of an ordeal than they had expected.

So far as Steve was concerned, the questions asked by the Coroner dealt solely with the matter of his arrival at the house, his discovery of Mrs. Kirby's body.

Ann's testimony confirmed all his statements. She had been alarmed by certain sounds from the floor below, had come downstairs to find Mr. Ransom in the morning room, whereupon they had at once called up a doctor, notified the police.

To Steve's astonishment, neither of them was asked regarding a plot to steal Mrs. Kirby's pearls; Parsons, the footman who had overheard their absurd conversation was not even placed on the witness stand.

Steve glanced somewhat uneasily at the Inspector. Why had this testimony been withheld? The expression on Duveen's face, however, told him nothing.

The police, it seemed, were ready to accept a perfunctory verdict, not having had time to develop a satisfactory case.

He smiled at Ann, sitting next to him, pressed her hand. It seemed incredible that less than three days had passed since he had first set foot in Halfway House . . . had stood admiring a clump of blue hydrangeas! So much had happened since that time . . . two sudden deaths . . . and the birth within him of something quite as important . . . something akin to life itself. He wondered if Ann felt the same way about it.

Edward, the fragile old butler, was telling his story. Of Mrs. Kirby's late visitor, whom he had glimpsed from an upstairs window. A woman, wearing a long, dark coat, whose face he had not seen. None of the other servants were able to corroborate his statement; they had been in bed. Then Jean Kirby was on the stand, pale as alabaster, telling of her presence at de Zara's apartment, her late arrival at the house. To Steve's surprise, not only the Count, but Georgette Masson, her mother's ex-maid, confirmed her statements. The three of them had been together, at de Zara's studio, from eleven until after twelve. Why? The Count lied like a gentleman to explain that; the Masson woman had come asking for an engagement as personal maid, when Miss Kirby did him the honor to become his wife.

All very innocuous, very respectable. Senator Kirby, the rugged statesman, snapped out his answers grudgingly. He had left home immediately after dinner . . . had joined his friend and legal advisor, Mr. Reed, at the latter's house. Later, they had gone for a drive . . . as Mr. Reed, at his elbow, promptly testified. No mention of a third member of their party; the Coroner was not disposed to probe. Steve smiled to himself; politics was a marvelous game. Again he glanced at Duveen, but the Inspector might have been a wooden Indian.

The greatest surprise of all, Steve thought, was the complete suppression of everything having to do with the Cannes photograph. Duveen's testimony regarding his call to Halfway House, the events that followed, made no mention of it. There was, perhaps, a good reason for that. To produce the picture now, before a clear case had been built up, would have served only to infuriate Senator Kirby, blacken his dead wife's name, and put the guilty person or persons on guard. Apparently the Inspector did not intend to have the case turned over to the newspapers. A clever egg, the Inspector . . . honest.

Most men weren't. After five minutes of deliberation, the jury brought in the usual indeterminate verdict.

Steve forced his way through the swarm of reporters surrounding Duveen, wondering what, if anything, the Inspector had up his sleeve. Luke Reed, shaking hands with the Coroner, showed all his sharp teeth in a vivid smile. Invisible wires had no doubt been pulled; the whole affair had gone off like a well-rehearsed bit of drama. Only the newspaper men were dissatisfied.

Inspector Duveen glanced at Steve down his stubborn nose.

"Doing anything this evening, young fellow?" he inquired.

"Nothing in particular," Steve said, glancing at Ann. "Why?"

"I want to see you. Come around to my office after dinner. Say at seven-thirty. Or a quarter to eight. Some points I'd like to go over."

"All right," Steve agreed. "I'm going in town anyway . . . back to my hotel." He met Duveen's eyes, found them inscrutable. "Anything wrong?"

"Not that I know of."

"Did you see Mrs. Mitchell?"

The Inspector withdrew still further behind his mask. "A very charming woman," he said. Abruptly he turned away, stopped to speak to one of his men. Steve stared after him for a moment, bewildered, then went up to Jean Kirby, standing not far away, with Ann.

"You've been very kind, Miss Kirby," he said.

"Are you going?" Ann asked.

"Yes. To my hotel. The Inspector wants to see me, this evening. I'll come out after breakfast tomorrow and honk my horn. There's something I want to talk over with you."

"Another play?" Ann's grin was deliberate. "I hope this time," she went on, under her breath, "it isn't a tragedy."

"Not a bit of it. Or a comedy either." Steve was very serious. "Just a nice, wholesome domestic drama; the kind that always makes a hit at the box office. Home and mother stuff."

"It's a popular subject," Ann said. "I trust you have the ability to make it interesting." She put her arm about Jean Kirby, moved away. "Be seeing you," she called over her shoulder.

Steve went into the house. Common politeness demanded that he should say good-bye to his host. He found Senator Kirby in his study with Luke Reed: both seemed in a dangerous humor.

"I want to thank you for your hospitality, Senator," Steve said.

Mr. Reed glared at him. The Senator spoke, gruffly.

"Let us hope, Mr. Ransom," he said, "that you will respect it."

"I don't understand, sir." Steve felt his cheeks growing red.

"I think you do." The Senator's manner was arrogant. "The police are quite able to look after their affairs, without the assistance of amateurs." He turned his back, spoke to Luke Reed.

Steve went out to his car, raging. Some newspaper men crowded about him, eager for a story. He pushed them aside, got into his car, drove off. Had Reed been telling the Senator of his, Steve's, activities in the case? It seemed probable. But why resent them, if he and Kirby had nothing to conceal? There were, of course, political repercussions . . . the fear of a scandal.

Still fuming over Senator Kirby's rudeness, Steve went to his room and changed. Before seeing the Inspector, he would have to get a bite to eat. He had just pulled on his coat when the telephone bell rang.

"Hello?" he asked.

"Dr. Badouine calling," the clerk at the desk said.

"Send him right up!" Steve was overjoyed. He had planned, all day, to see the doctor, but his trip to town, the inquest, later, had prevented it. Something told him that Dr. Badouine, could he be induced to talk, might supply the key to the mystery of both Mrs. Kirby's death, and that of Lawrence Dane. He awaited the psycho-analyst's coming impatiently.

XXI

Detective Sergeant Hunter in certain respects resembled a bull-dog; when his jaws closed on anything he held his grip indefinitely. It was an admirable quality.

For two hours he questioned the neighbors of Halfway House, hoping to find someone who had seen a stream-lined grey sedan in the narrow lane, on the night of Mrs. Kirby's murder.

Just when he thought his investigations would prove fruitless, he struck a promising clue.

The Negro butler of a house nearby had gone to the corner, at half-past eleven, to post some letters.

On his way back, he remembered having seen a grey car, turning into the lane at the east side of Halfway House.

He had not taken the number of it; there seemed no reason why he should. Nor had its presence attracted his particular attention. All he could tell Hunter, with any certainty, was that the car had been there, in the lane, at a little after eleven-thirty; he was sure of the time, because he had heard a clock, as he left the house, strike the half hour. His walk to the corner and back could not have taken over five minutes.

Hunter returned to Halfway House, not satisfied. A car in the lane meant nothing, unless it was shown to be Ransom's grey sedan. He went up to the machine, standing alongside the curb. It had not been used since the night before; Mr. Ransom and the Vickery girl had driven in town with Inspector Duveen.

Hunter opened the door. He had gone over the car very thoroughly on the night of Mrs. Kirby's murder, without results. Stubbornly, mechanically, he began another search.

Nothing in the pockets . . . nothing under either the front or rear seat cushions. In the small dashboard compartment was a pair of wadded black gloves. Woman's gloves, Hunter noted; they had not been there when he examined the car before. He took them out, stiffened suddenly as he noticed something unusual about one of the fingers. A slender object had been stuffed into it . . . slender and round.

Very carefully Hunter worked the object free, avoiding contact with his fingers. A slim glass vial, about the diameter of a lead pencil, and perhaps two inches long. Corked, with a drop or two of some colorless liquid still remaining in the bottom of it.

With a contented smile, Hunter wrapped the tiny bottle in his handkerchief, got into his car. The Chief had put it up to him to produce some real evidence against the Vickery girl and her boy friend; he believed he had that evidence now. The poison used to murder Lawrence Dane. Poured into his bottle of whiskey at the theatre. Miss Vickery had been in the car around nine-thirty the night before. But why had she kept the empty bottle? Why had she not thrown it away?

Hunter pondered that question endlessly throughout his drive to Police Headquarters. Did it mean that the girl was acting independently, without Ransom's knowledge? Had she, sitting there beside him, worked the tiny vial into one of her glove fingers, because she did not dare toss it from the car for fear her action might be observed? In

that case, why leave her gloves behind? The argument did
not seem very sound. Nor did it explain how the girl could
have left the car, gone into the theatre without her companion knowing why she had done so. It seemed unlikely.
Unless . . .

At Headquarters, Inspector Duveen proved to be out.
Hunter examined the gloves. Small, delicately perfumed.
Comparatively new. His eyes glowed as he saw inked
inside both of them the tiny initials, "A. V."

"That settles it!" he muttered and went up to the laboratory.

"See if you guys can find out what was in this bottle,
Joe," he said to a grey-haired man squinting at a test tube.
"It ought to be aconitine. There aren't any fingerprints."

XXII

The doctor came into the room, smiling but obviously tired. There was no lack of fire, however, Steve noticed, in his keen, intelligent eyes.

"Hard day," he said, dropping into a chair.

"Drink?" Steve went toward the telephone.

"No, thanks. I'll be all right, as soon as I have my dinner. Been tied up since noon on a most distressing case. Homicidal mania. Developed overnight. One of my best patients . . . a young girl I thought on the highroad to recovery. You never can tell what obscure complexes are lying dormant in such unbalanced minds; the poor creature tried to stab her own mother with a pair of garden shears. Quite mad, I'm afraid."

"Dreadful!" Steve nodded. "I looked for you, at the inquest."

"The Coroner didn't need me; the Medical Examiner's testimony was sufficient. I stopped by Halfway House, after leaving the hospital, saw Miss Vickery; she told me you'd lit out for your hotel, bag and baggage. What was the trouble, may I ask?"

"No trouble." Steve laughed. "I just couldn't feel happy any longer under Senator Kirby's large but inhospitable roof . . . the old crab! Annoyed, I think, by my humble activities in the case. Or he may have a guilty conscience."

183

"Anything new about Dane's death? I see the newspapers called it suicide, from the evidence. Is that the
police view?"

"I should say not. Dane was murdered. Somebody poisoned his whiskey, and later on switched bottles. Very
clever . . . only, the murderer forgot about corkscrews . . .
and corks. By the use of my superior intelligence," Steve
went on, grinning, "I was able to put our friend Duveen
on the right track." He explained the matter briefly.

"Amazing!" the doctor exclaimed, regarding Steve with
a look of admiration. "Never should have thought of it.
What a pity we stopped to let you smoke that cigarette,
after the second act; if we had arrived at Dane's dressing
room a few minutes earlier, we might have surprised the
murderer changing bottles . . . caused his, or her, arrest.
Queer, Mrs. Mitchell being there in the theatre. Do the
police suspect her?"

"I don't know. Duveen had a talk with her, I believe;
he may tell me the results when I see him, after dinner
tonight. All he said at the inquest was that he thought her
a very charming woman."

Dr. Badouine gave a somewhat cynical laugh.

"So does Senator Kirby. The lady must have hidden
charms. And of course most men would rather condemn
another man, than a woman. Especially an attractive
woman. Instinctive desire to protect the so-called weaker
sex. Not a bit weaker, really. Stronger, in many ways. One
of them is a ruthless ability to make use of this imaginary
weakness, to obtain all sorts of privileges, concessions,
from men. Duveen is only human."

"Didn't know you were a misogynist," Steve said.

"Lord, no . . . far from it." The doctor chuckled. "As
a matter of fact I happen to be in love myself, right now.
With a very charming woman. But as a wife likely to prove

expensive. Most charming women are, I think. However, that is neither here nor there. Who is your latest suspect, if not Mrs. Mitchell?" The doctor cocked a slightly ironical eye. "I hope you do better than we did yesterday."

"Don't ask me," Steve groaned. "That's up to the police. My personal choice would be Senator Kirby. Helped, no doubt, by his lawyer and man of all work, Luke Reed. If I ever saw a poisonous little reptile, he's it."

Dr. Badouine sat for several moments staring out of the window. Suddenly he straightened his tired shoulders.

"Mr. Ransom," he said, "I'm going to tell you something that perhaps I shouldn't, but it can do Mrs. Kirby no harm now, poor woman, and may help to discover her murderer. The constant dread that she lived under . . . a fear complex which was slowly undermining her entire nervous system, her health, arose from a belief that her husband intended to kill her, in order to marry again. It was more than a mere belief; she assured me that he had actually tried to take her life on at least two occasions.

"What?" Steve gasped. "Why . . . when you tell Duveen that . . . !"

"But I can't tell Duveen," the doctor interrupted. "Such communications between physician and patient are privileged. They can't be brought into court. And in this case, perhaps, merely the ramblings of a troubled and neurotic mind. I mention the matter to you, because you think Senator Kirby may be guilty; if he is, you will have to find other and more positive proof. As for what I have just told you, please keep it to yourself."

"Right," Steve said. "I shall. But at least it confirms my impression that Kirby is quite capable of having committed the crime. Although not of having disguised himself as a woman . . . he's far too big."

"Still," the doctor went on quietly, "that objection would not apply to Mr. Reed. He is, you may have noticed, a very small man, smooth-shaven, with almost effeminate hands and feet."

"Hell's fire," Steve exclaimed, "that's right!"

"Also, quite unscrupulous enough, I imagine, to commit any skullduggery, even murder, in the interests of the Senator's political career. With Mrs. Kirby out of the way, her husband can now marry Mrs. Mitchell, after a decent interval, without sacrificing the respect of the public. To have done so, in the face of a nasty divorce scandal, would have ruined him, politically . . . killed his future. And, from what I hear, he has large ambitions. A cabinet post, perhaps, if his party is successful in the coming elections. Even an eye on the White House."

Steve gave a shrill whistle.

"The idea," he said, "certainly has its possibilities! Reed may have come to the house disguised as a woman . . . tried to make Mrs. Kirby listen to reason . . . failed . . . killed her . . . escaped to join the Senator and Mrs. Mitchell, waiting in their car. That would give him a good alibi! And last night, Reed was there in a box at the theatre."

"With every reason for a second murder if Dane saw Mrs. Mitchell steal the photograph."

"In that case," Steve said, "it was probably Mrs. Mitchell who came to see Mrs. Kirby. I don't mean she killed her . . . you see, we've got to explain the presence of those bonds in Mrs. Kirby's safe . . . but she may have shown up with the snapshot, tried by means of it to compel a divorce. Mrs. Kirby comes back with an offer to buy the picture, for a couple of hundred thousand bucks. No sale. The two women have a row. Mrs. Mitchell chokes, silences her . . . runs off. That would be about eleven-thirty. Joins Reed and the Senator, waiting outside. They don't dare leave things that way; knowing that as soon as Mrs. Kirby comes to she will talk. So Reed, or the Senator, or both, go back and finish the operation."

"Certainly logical," Dr. Badouine agreed. "All except leaving the photograph behind. Still, the two men may have thought Mrs. Mitchell had it. Or used the thing as a red herring across the trail to confuse the bloodhounds of the law!" The doctor laughed, a bit harshly. "Just because we can't imagine Kirby leaving that picture makes it, psychologically, one of the safest things he could do. It points straight to de Zara as the murderer, and but for what may well be a manufactured alibi, the Count still remains our most logical suspect."

"Why?" Steve asked quickly. "Kirby had just as strong a motive."

"No. Not as strong. A woman . . . yes. But with de Zara, not only a woman, but a fortune of twenty millions, as soon as he and Miss Kirby are married. In the long run he stands to gain far more, by Mrs. Kirby's death, than anyone else."

Steve sat for a moment, thinking. Of de Zara's small, round-bladed stiletto, so carefully replaced to hide the dust-silhouette on the wall. Of the Count's presence, with a slim, dark woman, so near the theatre the night before. Of the wrapped bottle, that might have contained whiskey . . . Scotch whiskey . . . under his arm. The ringing of the telephone bell brought him back to realities.

He picked up the instrument, heard Ann's voice; it sounded, he thought, a bit unnatural, strained.

"Hello, honey!" he said. "Anything wrong?"

"No, Steve . . . nothing wrong." The unexpected use of his first name thrilled him. "Only . . . I think I've found out what Mrs. Kirby meant . . . about . . . about a nail!"

"What?" Steve exclaimed; his voice made the transmitter rattle.

"I can't tell you . . . now." Ann was whispering. "I'd rather not speak of it . . . mention names . . . over the telephone. The whole thing is too . . . incredible. I want to talk to you, first. Can you come out here, after dinner?"

"Of course! The minute I get through with Duveen; he expects me at his office, around a quarter to eight. But this sounds mighty important . . ."

"It is. Still, it will keep until you get here."

"Tell you what you do," Steve said. "I won't darken the Senator's doorway, little one. Not after the way he treated me this afternoon. Stephen Ransom may be a worm, but he still has his pride. When you finish dinner, beat it down to that stone bench in the garden. You know . . . the one by the lily pond. Wait there, and think of me. I don't know how long I'll be with Duveen, but I'll join you as soon as I can make it . . . say around nine o'clock. Right? And take care of yourself, sweetness. You're sure, are you, about this nail business?"

"So sure," Ann replied, in a small, somewhat terrified voice, "that I think I can tell you who the murderer was. You come out. I don't dare talk any longer now." He heard the receiver click into place.

"Anything new?" the doctor asked, as Steve turned from the telephone. "You seem upset."

"New? My God!" Steve sank into a chair. "You remember those words Mrs. Kirby called out just before she was choked, murdered? Something about a nail."

"Very well. We discussed it, if I am not mistaken. My thought was she had accused someone of blackmail."

"Miss Vickery just telephoned me she's got the answer. What do you think about that?"

"Remarkable," the doctor nodded, "assuming she is right."

"I'd have my doubts, with most women," Steve went on. "But not Ann Vickery. When she says a thing, I pay attention to it."

"So I have observed." Dr. Badouine gave Steve an amused smile. "And what is her explanation?"

"She didn't tell me. Wouldn't, over the telephone. Wants me to come out . . . says she can name the murderer."

"You are going, of course?"

"Of course. As soon as I get through with Duveen."

The doctor rose, picked up his hat, nodding.

"I should not be surprised," he said, "if what Miss Vickery has discovered bears out the information I have just given you, regarding Senator Kirby. Those homicidal attacks on his wife. I shall be tremendously interested to hear what she has to say. Why not stop by at my house on your way downtown? I expect to be at home all evening; we might have a drink, a little chat."

"It's a date," Steve said.

XXIII

The Inspector was late in returning to his office at Headquarters; he had spent a futile hour, at the theatre, questioning the doorkeeper, stage crew, the call boy. Hunter was waiting for him, a pair of gloves, a small glass bottle, in his hands.

"Thought I better see you, Chief," he said, "before you talked to that Ransom guy; he's waiting outside."

"I know." The Inspector nodded. "What's on your mind?"

Hunter laid the gloves, the bottle, on Duveen's desk, explained where he had found them.

"You wanted evidence," he said. "I got it. Aconitine in the bottle; here's the laboratory report. Miss Vickery's initials on the gloves! Dead open and shut. Looks to me like the two of them better be given the works."

Inspector Duveen stared at the desk-top, frowning. He was not satisfied; the case looked too open and shut.

"Could have been planted," he said. "That car's been standing out in front of the Senator's house ever since Ransom brought it back last night."

"Pollock was on duty; he'd of seen anybody go near it."

"Ought to have."

"I found someone, works two doors away, says he noticed a streamlined grey sedan in that lane alongside the

191

Kirby place at half-past eleven, the night the old lady was murdered."

"Lots of grey sedans," Duveen replied. "Our friend Luke Reed has one."

Hunter was annoyed at the Inspector's lack of enthusiasm.

"What's the idea, Chief?" he said. "Got some dope I haven't heard about?"

"No, Sam!" Duveen crashed his fist on the desk-top. "I wish I had. But use your bean. We figured Dane a suicide. Not a scrap of evidence to show anything different. Then Ransom comes along and gives it to us. Would a murderer do that? He would not!"

"Maybe the girl worked the whole thing alone. Killed Mrs. Kirby before Ransom got there, planted the photograph, hid the pearls, ran back upstairs when she heard his car. That would explain how the bottle came to be in the glove tip . . . she shoved it in there so Ransom wouldn't see it. She was right near the theatre, at the time that woman came in."

"How could she get out of the car, without Ransom knowing it? Be yourself."

"Maybe she wasn't in the car. Maybe she did it while Ransom was up in his room at the hotel, packing his bag. He had to leave her, didn't he, so he could check out? They didn't get home until nine-forty-five. Could do it in a quarter of an hour. There's ten, fifteen, minutes, to be accounted for somehow. I think the girl's guilty as hell."

Duveen stared at the gloves without seeing them; he felt intuitively, that some vital clue in the case had so far eluded him, been completely missed.

"All right, Sam," he said wearily. "You've done mighty good work. Send Ransom in here."

Steve entered the office, bubbling over with enthusiasm. He did not see the frown on Duveen's face.

"Miss Vickery telephoned me just before dinner, Chief," he announced, "that she's found out what Mrs. Kirby meant by 'The nail!'"

"Has she?" The Inspector said dryly. "I came across a possible explanation of it myself, talking to Mrs. Mitchell. What's Miss Vickery's idea?"

"She wouldn't tell me. I'm going out to the house as soon as I leave here."

"Before you go there are some questions I'll have to ask you." Duveen picked up the gloves. "One of my men found these, this morning, in your car."

"Sure. Why not? Miss Vickery left them there last night, when I drove her home. I put them in the dashboard compartment."

"This bottle," Duveen went on, his voice harsh as ashes, "was found stuck in the finger of one of them. It still has a little poison . . . aconitine . . . in the bottom of it."

Steve leaped from his chair, faced the Inspector in a sudden rage.

"Somebody must have planted it there!" he shouted. "The dirty son of a . . ."

"Pipe down!" Duveen waved his stumpy hand. "You have anyone in that car last night, except Miss Vickery?"

"No one! Not a soul! Look here, Inspector . . . I just thought of something. Count de Zara was dining at the hotel, with a woman last night. They went out a little after nine. A tall, dark woman! He said she was the wife of a friend, he was taking to the station! He had a bottle, wrapped up, under his arm. It might have been whiskey to replace the poisoned one."

Duveen managed to check the furious outburst. "Keep your shirt on!" he said. "No use getting excited; I'm not accusing anybody . . . yet."

"But," Steve insisted, "my car was parked outside the theatre for half an hour, last night! Nothing to prevent de Zara, or that woman, from planting the poison bottle in those gloves."

"Nothing, except that he took her to the station, put her on a train, just as he said. I had a man tailing him."

"Then it must have been done later, after I drove the car back to Halfway House."

"I had a man on watch outside, all night."

"He couldn't have kept his eyes on the car every minute! It was dark . . . my God!"

Duveen's head jerked up. Steve was standing rigid, an expression of terror on his face.

"What's the matter?" the Inspector said, eyeing him in surprise.

"Don't you see?" He glanced at his watch. "Miss Vickery telephoned me, before dinner, that she knew what Mrs. Kirby meant by those words she called out, just before she was murdered! Said she could tell me the murderer's name! Suppose someone overheard her! There are extension phones all over the place! Senator Kirby . . . Luke Reed . . . he was on hand for dinner . . . Miss Kirby . . . even if she isn't guilty herself she might tip off the Count! The servants . . . I don't trust that fellow Parsons. And I told Miss Vickery, poor kid, to go down in the garden and wait for me there; because I didn't feel welcome in Senator Kirby's house! She's sitting on that bench in the dark right now, all ready for the murderer to creep up and finish her! Before she has a chance to tell me what she knows! I don't even dare telephone! Can't be sure who would get the message . . . they'd have to send for her . . . might only precipitate matters! Hell!" He picked up his hat, ran to the door. "I'm going out there! Now! Should have gone before! The fact that the empty poison bottle must have been planted in my machine during the night proves that the murderer is someone at Halfway House!"

Inspector Duveen leaped from his desk; his cool blue eyes were suddenly blazing.

"I'm going with you!" he said. "In my car, then we won't have to worry about traffic lights!"

XXIV

Ann put down the telephone, went to the door of the library. She had spoken in a very low voice, little more than a whisper; it seemed certain that no one could have overheard her, even had they stood at the other end of the big, silent room.

Her feet made no sound, on the deep-piled Eastern rugs. Down the long hall she saw Edward, the butler, coming toward her from the direction of the morning room; it was equipped with a telephone extension but she had no reason to feel suspicious of Edward . . . to suppose that he had been listening . . . no more reason than to suspect anyone else, in this dim and oppressive old house.

At the other end of the corridor was Senator Kirby's study; he was closeted there now, Ann knew, with Luke Reed. That room, too, had a telephone extension. Had either of the two men overheard what she had just confided to Steve? She could hear them talking, and could distinguish the Senator's loud, sonorous voice, above Mr. Reed's shrill, piping one.

It would be a relief, Ann felt, to get away from this dismal place. Both its century-old murder and its more recent harrowing crime seemed to hold the threat of further tragedies to come.

She laughed at her premonitions, turned into the central hall. Jean Kirby was slowly descending the stairs. The girl had doubtless been in her own private suite on the floor above, also equipped with a telephone. She came down the steps like an automaton, holding herself erect with conscious effort. Her face, bloodless, was set in rigid lines, but her eyes were mobile, and unnaturally brilliant. Scarcely noticing Ann as she passed her, Jean went into the library, closed the door.

Ann gazed after her, surprised. The girl, of course, was suffering intensely from the shock of her mother's tragic death, the unpleasant experience of the inquest, but Ann could not shake off the feeling that Jean Kirby's manner had for some reason become less friendly. Then Edward was tapping at the door of the Senator's study, announcing that dinner was served.

It was the first meal that the family had eaten together since the night of Mrs. Kirby's murder, and Ann shivered, certain that it would be a ghastly one. Tomorrow, thank God, she would be out of it all . . . would be on her way back to New York. With a curious, sinking sensation about her heart she went into the large, oak-paneled dining room, stood waiting for the others to appear.

Jean Kirby joined her almost at once, white and impassive; a moment later Luke Reed and the Senator came in. No one spoke; it was, Ann thought, like a scene from some dark and gloomy pantomime. She sat down, repressing a sudden impulse to scream.

Parsons, the second man, moving as silently as a spirit figure, placed a pink crescent of melon before her, while Edward, his fragile hand trembling, poured sherry into her glass. Ann drank the mellow wine gratefully, feeling the need of stimulation.

At the far end of the table Senator Kirby and Luke Reed conversed in rumbling whispers, discussing some political issue. The Senator had never made a pretense of deep affection for his wife; he showed no evidences of grief now. The harsh, bony planes of his face, grey and inscrutable, might have been cut from trap-rock; only his eyes, flicking from time to time about the table, betrayed his agitation. Something was disturbing him powerfully, Ann saw . . . something akin to fear.

Luke Reed's expression, on the contrary, was almost childishly bland; the little lawyer nodded and smirked as though nothing disturbed him, nothing more serious than the proper seasoning of his soup, or the state of the weather. That, Ann knew, was an even more impenetrable mask than the stony visage presented by Senator Kirby; at least one could see that the Senator was disturbed. In Mr. Reed's case nothing was revealed; his expression registered an absolute zero.

Across the table, Jean Kirby forced down her food mechanically, staring at her plate. Perhaps the vacant chair at her left, facing the Senator's, was what kept them all so grimly silent. For the first time in her life Ann realized the dreadful emptiness that death can bring; that vacant chair was, in a way, the most vital and eloquent thing in the room; far more so than any of the four who sat there at the table.

At last the ordeal came to an end. Ann set her coffee cup back into its saucer with a rattle that showed how her fingers were shaking, watched Jean rise, eager for the moment when she might escape to the garden. Edward was serving cigars and brandy, in the library; Ann waited until the Senator and Mr. Reed had left the dining room, then went into the east-wing corridor. She was almost running as she reached the flagstone terrace.

It was darker, outside, than she had expected, and even here, in the fresh, cool air she could not shake off the feeling of oppression under which she had labored throughout dinner. A premonition of danger which even the scent of freshly clipped grass, the perfume of syringa and lilacs, did nothing to relieve.

She stood for a moment on the terrace. There was no moon; the night sky was like indigo velvet, dusted with pale stars. Before her stretched the double line of box trees; their dense, black foliage might have been carved from ebony, it seemed so rigid, still. With a laugh at her fears Ann ran swiftly between them, her feet scarcely touching the widely spaced flags. She was anxious to reach the small stretch of open lawn surrounding the bench, the lily pond; it was not so dark, there.

Her eyes, accustomed now to the change in light, made out the long stone bench; it suggested, she thought with a shudder, a shadowy tomb. There were flower beds at either side of it, and beyond them, the circular marble rim of the pool. She sat down to wait, her heart pounding a little . . . hoped she would not have to wait long. The ordeal at the dinner table had been endless; Steve might appear at any moment now.

It astonished, even amused her a little, to realize how eager she was to have him with her. Not only to tell him what she had discovered, but to feel that he was there, at her side. It was a new experience, so far as she was concerned, a new emotion. Hitherto no one man had mattered that much in her rather busy life. Plenty of friends, of course, with whom she dined, danced, went to parties, shows, but none of them had been . . . she tried to think of an adequate word . . . essential. That was it . . . essential. The ones she knew were not necessities, but luxuries, like the cocktails and caviar they bought her, the tickets for operas, plays. Now, for some mysterious reason, this particular and not very unusual male, with the humorous eyes and rusty brown hair had become necessary for her happiness and her well-being. Ann laughed at the thought of it, even though she knew it to be true. So this, it seemed, was love. A mysterious and quite unreasonable process by which two ordinary, everyday people, not materially different from all the rest, suddenly found themselves essential to each other. Perhaps it was just a biological trick, but even so she found it a very pleasant one. She sat on the bench for a long time.

Preoccupation . . . a glamorous dream. It prevented her from hearing the almost noiseless footsteps on the soft, green turf . . . from seeing the shadow that moved among the deeper shadows along the line of box. She did not know of its presence until two arms slid over her shoulders, with muscular fingers at the end of them closing about her neck.

To spring forward was automatic; Ann did so with such swift violence that she almost escaped those clutching hands. Almost, but not quite. One of them caught at her shoulder, whirled her about as she attempted to run toward the house. Instantly the other was again at her throat. She was aware of a figure bending over her . . . a woman, wearing a long, dark coat. Taller than herself . . . stronger . . . with bright, terrible eyes . . . a cruel, passion-twisted face! She tried to scream, struggling against those muscular hands, fighting desperately for breath! Everything seemed to be growing dimmer, flickering out, like a dying electric bulb, a guttering candle! Enormous drums were beating, thundering in her ears! Then blackness, in which there was no sensation at all! No knowledge of sensation! No wish for it! Oblivion!

XXV

Steve Ransom scarcely spoke during that furious ten-minute drive; he spent the time alternately pressing his knees against the dashboard, and cursing himself for not having gone to the house at once. Criminal stupidity . . . no less!

"I knew," he muttered once, between hard, twisting lips, "that Senator Kirby tried to kill his wife, before!"

"How?" Duveen asked, intent on his driving.

Steve did not answer him. They were approaching the house, now.

"The side lane!" he said. "That's nearest to the bench where I told her to wait. My God, it's dark!"

Except for a faint sky-glow the garden was a mass of shadows, vague and uncertain. Steve was out of the car even before it stopped . . . was hurling himself over the low stone wall. With Duveen close behind him, he raced down the box-lined path.

Ahead of them a woman screamed. Her voice, shrill with terror was instantly smothered, stopped. In the open space at the end of the walk two dim figures were struggling. Two women; their shadowy outlines told that much. One of them fell, crashing heavily against the long stone bench . . . the other whirled off through the darkness.

Steve dropped to his knees, scarcely realizing that the Inspector almost tripped over him as he vanished in quick pursuit.

"Ann!" he whispered, close to sobbing. Her white, still face against his shoulder was what he had dreaded to see, all through that thundering drive.

Always, after that night, the heavy, sick-sweet fragrance of hyacinths made Steve Ransom physically ill. Beds of the wax-like flowers circled each end of the bench before which Ann's body lay.

Always, the keen odor of the flowers brought to his mind pictures of the garden . . . not sharp, vivid pictures, filled with detail, but cloudy visions, in deep shadow, like the place itself. Only the white face of the girl, staring sightlessly up into his own, stood out with any distinctness, and even that seemed a grotesque, impossible mask.

Before him stretched the ancient lovers' lane, leading to Halfway House; lighted windows at the end of it made golden arabesques through the surrounding shrubbery.

Behind lay the sweep of the garden, dotted with bushes in serried black clumps. From among them came the thud of running feet, faint and smothered, because of the soft, springy turf. Inspector Duveen, in pursuit of the woman who had darted away so swiftly upon their approach. The only other sound was a tremulous piping of tree-frogs, against a distant hum of city traffic. Darkness . . . silence . . . the heavy perfume of hyacinths . . . the wax-like pallor of Ann's staring face! Those were the impressions that crowded Steve's brain, during the fraction of a second that elapsed as he knelt down, took the girl in his arms.

His left hand, under her head, was wet . . . sticky wet. Blood, he realized at once, groaning. She was not dead . . . the faint, almost imperceptible rise and fall of her breasts told him that. But the cry she had given as they raced

toward her had been abruptly smothered, choked . . . by
a hard grip on her throat. A murderous grip. No reason
for blood, from that cause . . . no reason for her present
death-like immobility! There must be another . . . a frac-
tured skull, perhaps, produced as she was flung backward
against the marble bench, the hard stone flags beneath.

Now he was carrying her toward the house. Stagger-
ing a little, not from the weight of his burden but from
a guilty fear that help for the girl might have come too
late. It was a very precious burden; only at that desperate
moment did Steve realize how precious . . . one to be
hand-led gently, lest some awkward slip or jar might leave
her suddenly dead in his arms.

Before him rose the amber oblongs of the French windows; he had entered the morning room through one of
them, ages before, it seemed now, to find Mrs. Kirby dead.
Who would have thought that only three nights later . . . ?

Someone was in the room. A woman. Tall, slender,
dressed in black. Jean Kirby. Her face was grey like old
silver, tarnished, as she peered through the small, square
panes.

Steve kicked against the window frame. Violently. He
did not speak. In this house were potential enemies. A
murderer, perhaps . . . or those who arranged to have murder done, for their safety, their ultimate benefit. That
made no difference, now; even murderers would not dare
refuse him aid.

Jean Kirby opened the window, staring. Her eyes were
dark with fear.

"Oh!" she whispered, forcing out the words almost mechanically as she saw at a glance the limp figure in Steve's
arms. "Oh . . . Mr. Ransom! What . . . what has happened?"

Steve strode into the room, brushing the girl aside in
his haste.

"Call the nearest doctor!" he exclaimed. "Life or death! And tell me where Miss Vickery's room is!" Jean Kirby ran ahead of him into the hall.

"The first door at the head of the stairs!" she said, pointing. "I'll get Dr. Hall, he's close." She darted away.

Steve climbed the endless steps, sweat in his eyes. From his feelings, he might have been sweating blood. A precious stream of it, warm and terrifying, dripped slowly down his wrist, his arm. He turned the knob of the door awkwardly with the hand supporting Ann's sagging knees, lurched into the bedroom. Thank God for the small reading lamp, casting a faint circle of light over the turned-down sheets. He had not put a woman to bed before . . . at least not a woman with whom he was in love. As he lowered her inert body red drops appeared on the counterpane; a bright crimson stain grew against the lace-edged pillows. Frantically he tried to check the flow of blood with his handkerchief.

There was nothing to be done, but wait. Only a physician could be of any help, now. Ann's breathing, so faint before, was now scarcely perceptible; she seemed a woman dying, almost dead. Steve seized her wrist, desperately counting her rapid and fluttering heartbeats. He knew nothing of pulses, had never had occasion to take even his own. Now he could feel it plainly enough, confusing that of the girl, shaking his whole frame.

The door of the room was pushed open, and two figures came quickly in. Jean Kirby, whispering under her breath that Dr. Hall would arrive in a few moments. Inspector Duveen, staring at the unconscious girl on the bed, muttering angrily that the woman he had pursued had gotten away in a car . . . that because of the darkness he had been unable to secure the license number of it.

"I've sent out a call," he said to Steve, "but there's nothing to go on! A woman, in a car! Thousands of 'em! That won't get us anywhere!"

"No." Steve was still trying at staunch the flow of blood from Ann's head. "It won't. Anyway, it doesn't make much difference. Not now. Nothing does, except," he glanced at Ann's white face, "except Miss Vickery."

After that, a dull, terrifying silence, broken at last by the distant ringing of a bell.

"The doctor!" Jean Kirby said, hurrying from the room.

Inspector Duveen stood, a grim figure at the other side of the bed.

"This killer," he muttered, "is getting desperate. The poor kid's message to you was overheard."

"Where is Senator Kirby?" Steve said suddenly.

"Out. With Luke Reed. They left right after dinner, the butler tells me . . . didn't say where they were headed."

"That makes anything possible," Steve went on. "If we only knew what Miss Vickery had found out!" He glanced at Ann's still figure. "Inspector Duveen, we ought to be ashamed of ourselves! To let this poor youngster . . ."

"Yes," Duveen said. "I feel that way myself. But so help me God . . ."

A stir outside the door and the doctor, with Jean Kirby, came into the room. An elderly, tight-lipped man, silent with the silence of one whose words are important. He made a swift examination, called for boiling water.

"The young lady has been strangled," he announced. "She also has a bad scalp wound, a concussion of the brain. I do not think she is in any immediate danger, but absolute quiet, rest, are essential, of course. I shall send for a nurse . . ."

"How long?" the Inspector asked, "before she'll be able to talk? I'm Assistant Superintendent Duveen, of the Detective Bureau, doctor," he added.

"Not for many hours. Days, perhaps. She has undergone a severe and almost fatal shock." The physician scrubbed the white surface of Ann's forearm with a bit of moist cotton, inserted the needle of a hypodermic syringe. "The

greatest care will be necessary, if she is to recover. I suggest," he stared coldly from the Inspector to Steve Ransom, "that you gentlemen leave the room!"

Steve bent over, touched his lips to Ann's forehead.

"Of course," he said, rising. "Of course. And about the
nurse?"

"Miss Kirby will telephone for her. I shall remain with
the patient until help arrives."

He gave Jean a number. Ann Vickery began to speak,
then, broken, scarcely breathed words, unintelligible to
all those in the room except one.

"That nail!" she muttered, turning her head restlessly
as the doctor sponged the deep wound in her scalp . . .
"that crooked fingernail! Oh . . . Steve darling . . . look
out! So dangerous! So very dangerous! Oh . . . It hurts . . .
It hurts . . . "

Steve Ransom, at the door, drew back his shoulders.
Understanding grew in his furious eyes.

"You'll stay here with her, doctor?" he muttered. "You
won't leave her alone?"

"Of course not! I shouldn't think of it . . ." The doctor
glanced up with an impatient frown.

Steve touched the Inspector's arm.

"Let's go!" he said harshly. "I know how to find the
murderer now!"

XXVI

"What's the idea," Inspector Duveen asked, jamming an impatient foot on the gas, "of stopping by Dr. Badouine's first? I've got to round up these suspects . . . get hold of Senator Kirby . . . Luke Reed . . . that Mitchell woman . . ."

"I promised the doctor," Steve said, "to let him know the results of our talk with Miss Vickery."

"What good will that do?" The Inspector regarded Steve doubtfully out of the corner of one eye. "You said you knew how to find the murderer. I take it from that you mean Mrs. Kirby started to yell what she did because whoever was trying to choke her had a crooked fingernail. If that's true, it ought to be easy enough to identify the killer."

Steve glanced down at the Inspector's right forefinger, outstretched along the rim of the steering wheel. The nail of it had been cut down to a blunt triangle by the splinter of shrapnel which had mangled the rest of his hand.

"Inspector Duveen," he said. "I'm no Sherlock Holmes. I don't pretend to know anything about detective work. But it seems to me that identifying the murderer by means of a malformed fingernail, without some additional proof isn't going to help us any. Our man . . . or woman . . . would probably say 'So what?' Just as you would," Steve went on, touching the Inspector's lean forefinger . . . "if somebody accused you."

"Right." Duveen shrugged his powerful shoulders. "You think Badouine can tell us something?"

"Yes," Steve said. "I think he can. Dr. Badouine is a very clever, a very intelligent man. I hope, when we see him, to find out why Mrs. Kirby cried out those peculiar words. And I'm going to ask him because I believe he can tell us what we want to know. If I'm right, you'll have more than a crooked fingernail to go on. If I'm wrong, there won't be much time lost."

Duveen grunted, whirling the car into K Street. The doctor's house was dimly lighted. Steve followed his companion up the steps, waited. A pleasant-faced Negro answered the bell.

"No, suh," he grinned, "the doctuh ain't in jes' now; got a call fum the hospittle 'round dinner time; he's been gone a right smart while. Reckon you all better come in and wait; he tole me he was expectin' a gen'man later."

"Right," Steve said. "We will."

"You'll find seats in here." The Negro ushered them into a waiting room. "Rest youh hats."

"Well," Duveen grumbled, staring about. "We got nothing but time."

Steve went to the rear of the room, pushed open a door.

"Consulting office, back there," he announced. "You know I've been here before. Secretary sits at this desk." He indicated an alcove between the two rooms. "I wonder where the doctor keeps his car."

"All these old houses have garages in back," Duveen said. "Stables, fixed over. What difference does it make where he keeps his car?"

"Not a bit, to me," Steve laughed, throwing himself into a chair. "I was just wondering if he'd be coming in the front way or the rear."

The immediate sharp closing of a door at the end of the hall, followed by quick footsteps, answered the question. Dr. Badouine, physician's bag in hand, was smiling at them from the open doorway.

"Hello, Ransom," he exclaimed, putting out his hand. "Hope I haven't kept you waiting too long. And you, Inspector! Did my man explain? I left word with him. That troublesome homicidal case, Ransom, I mentioned before. I'm a bit tired. Perhaps a dose of *spiritus frumenti* would do us all good. Simms," he called down the hall, "glasses, and a bowl of ice. Sit down, gentlemen. I'm very eager to hear what light Miss Vickery was able to throw on your murder problem, Inspector."

"Not much," Duveen said gloomily. "The poor girl has been very nearly murdered herself."

"What? You can't mean it. But . . . why? And by whom?" The doctor's luminous eyes blazed.

"By the murderer, I suppose," the Inspector went on. "To keep her from talking. But she did mutter a couple of words." He glanced at Steve.

"Do they afford any clue?"

"That is a question I want to ask you," Steve said. "Miss Vickery has a brain concussion. She may be unconscious, too ill to answer any questions, for some time. All she said, in her delirium, was 'That nail . . . that crooked fingernail.'"

"Fingernail?" Dr. Badouine's face showed complete surprise. "Then, if she really heard what she thinks, it would seem that Mrs. Kirby, at the moment of her death, was commenting on the shape of someone's fingernail."

"Of her murderer's fingernail, let us say," Steve corrected.

"Possibly. But why?"

"Because the person was disguised, and only the sudden sight of that peculiar nail caused Mrs. Kirby to recognize him! The moment she did, she must have cried out, at the same time clutching at his wig!"

"Of course," Dr. Badouine agreed, regarding the Inspector with a curious, questioning smile.

"The words that rushed to her lips," Steve went on, "and were overheard by Miss Vickery in the room above, came from anger, mixed with amazement, because this man she had so dramatically exposed was perhaps the last person in the world she expected to find trying to blackmail her! That swift anger caused her death; she was throttled before she could alarm the house, bring on him the ruin, the disgrace, his exposure would have caused."

Dr. Badouine nodded slowly, thoughtfully.

"The reconstruction seems to me logical," he said, "provided Miss Vickery actually heard any such words. Unfortunately we have only her statement to that effect, and while I do not mean to question the girl's veracity she might easily have been mistaken. My own thought was that Mrs. Kirby tried to say something like blackmail."

"Yes," Steve said. "I know."

"Granting, however, that your theory is right," Dr. Badouine went on, "I don't quite see the value of it, from an evidential standpoint. Many persons have misshapen fingernails, the result of accident, or disease. In fact, I happen to possess one myself." He held out a slim, well-manicured hand. "This index finger. I split the end of it when I was a boy, doing some carpentry work, and the wound, not properly cared for, healed badly . . . left a rough diagonal ridge across the nail. But it would be possible to find hundreds, even thousands, of persons in Washington with similar malformations, and yet be no nearer a solution of the problem of Mrs. Kirby's murder than before. Thank you, Simms." He turned to the Negro, entering the room with a tray. "Put it there on the table. I'll get the whiskey myself."

The servant put the tray down, went out. Inspector Duveen was nodding but he seemed puzzled.

"Was it your idea, Mr. Ransom," he said, "that Dr. Badouine could tell us something that would help identify Mrs. Kirby's murderer?"

"Yes." Steve's eyes met the doctor's somberly. "He could tell us, if Mrs. Kirby sat, day after day, across a desk talking to a man who had the habit of drumming on it with his finger tips, whether she wouldn't be likely to notice such a peculiar nail? And to recognize it, later on, if it happened to come suddenly to her attention?"

"Of course," the doctor replied. "Almost inevitably, I should say. But first, we must find such a man. And second, having found him, must prove, if we can, that the purely hypothetical train of events you have suggested actually took place. A most interesting speculation. I shall enjoy discussing it with you. But first, let us have our little drink; the ice is beginning to melt. I keep my fine whiskey under lock and key. In a closet adjoining my bedroom. Sit down, gentlemen, while I get a bottle; it will take me only a moment." He picked up his black leather bag, started for the hall.

"Wait a minute, doctor," Steve said harshly.

"Yes?" Dr. Badouine turned, smiling. "Anything I can do?"

"If you will. A moment ago you said that we must first find a man with a deformed fingernail whom Mrs. Kirby saw, talked to frequently, and second prove that this man, disguised as a woman, murdered her. I have a man in mind who fulfills perfectly the first conditions. Will you help me prove, or disprove, the second?"

"Why, certainly. But how can I?"

"By opening that satchel in your hand!" Steve pointed to the physician's black bag.

"But this is ridiculous." Dr. Badouine's suave face was suddenly red. "It contains only my medicines, my drugs."

"So I should suppose," Steve went on quietly, "and hence there is no reason why you should not open it."

"You are insulting, Mr. Ransom!"

"But . . . why? I said prove, or disprove, remember . . ."

"Nonsense!" Dr. Badouine stood suddenly at bay in the doorway, the satchel clutched firmly in his hand. "I am under no obligation to prove anything to you, certainly not what my medical bag contains. As for you, Inspector, I am sure you are too able and intelligent a police officer not to know that you cannot open this bag, or require me to open it, without a search warrant. I am sorry if I seem disobliging, but both as a physician and a man I resent Mr. Ransom's humiliating suspicions. Good night!" He started for the stairs. Inspector Duveen did not move to stop him.

"My God!" Steve groaned, "don't you know he'll burn it before you can get back with a warrant?"

"Can't do a thing," Duveen groaned. "That's the law. If you happened to be wrong . . ."

Steve wheeled on the doctor, now smiling at him from the foot of the stairs. His slow, ironic smile, mixed with a memory of Ann's deathly white face, exploded in Steve Ransom's brain like a torpedo. His left fist shot out, then his right, in the old familiar one-two. Dr. Badouine crashed against the newel post, hung over it, dazed. With a snarl of anger Steve tore open the bag.

"Here's your proof!" he exclaimed, hurling at the Inspector's feet a wig, a pair of satin ties, a velvet toque, a one-piece dress, a woman's black cloth coat, tightly rolled.

XXVII

Ann Vickery leaned back against the pillows of the big Du Barry bed. She felt thankful to be alive, especially on such a morning, so sweet and heady with the odors of spring. The air outside, still and very clear, was filled with innumerable sparks of sunshine, like the flecks of gold-leaf in a glass of *Eau de Vie de Dantzig*. Sweet and intoxicating. Especially to one somewhat weak after three pain-racked days in bed. She glanced at Steve, standing near the window and liked the fine dust of freckles over his nose.

Across the room Nicolas de Zara was sitting in a chair too small for him, holding Jean Kirby's hand. A giant, but rather of the story-book variety, Ann decided, huge, simple, good-natured. Jean, beside him, still looked like a marble Venus, but no longer new marble, chalk-white; there were warm tones in her cheeks that made Ann think, with a shudder, of the mellow Greek vase in which she had once set a cluster of blue hydrangeas! Since that tragic day a cloud of horror had enveloped Halfway House, dark and threatening; she hoped it was gone, now.

Beyond Jean and de Zara, Judge Tyson was chatting with Miss Webster, her nurse. No suggestion of tragedy showed itself in the Judge's pink and cherubic face; he was smiling at the girl like a whiskerless Santa Claus. Ann felt

215

her injured head: she herself had come closer to that horror than any of the others in the room. Closer to death . . .

The door suddenly opened and Senator Kirby, harsh
and bristling, stalked in; behind him came Inspector
Duveen.

The Inspector, to judge from his smile, felt at peace
with the world. Even with the Senator, in spite of their
recent differences. He nodded genially to the others, went
up to Ann and took her hand.

"Well, young woman," he said, "you were right; he's
confessed. How are you feeling this morning?"

"Fine," Ann said. "Although my head still hurts."

"Ought to." The Inspector grinned. "With seven stitch-
es in it. A close shave . . ."

"Yes." Ann's hand went to her bandages. "I'm glad these
keep you from seeing how close; I told the doctor I hoped
I'd have a few stray locks left."

"It will grow out." The Inspector sat on the edge of the
bed. "Feel equal to telling me how you knew, about that
fingernail? Of course I've always said a woman's guess . . ."

"It wasn't exactly a guess," Ann grinned. "Dr. Badouine came here, the day of the inquest, to see Mr. Ransom,
but he'd gone back to the hotel. The doctor and I talked,
in the garden. When I lit a cigarette he struck a match
for me, held it. With that crooked fingernail right under
my nose. So I thought, if *that* had been what Mrs. Kirby
meant," Ann hesitated, glancing at the Senator near the
foot of the bed, "that maybe Dr. Badouine . . ."

"Go on!" Kirby's sallow, gaunt face remained impassive. "We are here for that purpose."

"So I called up Mr. Ransom, at the hotel, and told
him a little, not much. I was afraid to mention names,
although I didn't know of course that Dr. Badouine had
gone to the hotel, was sitting right there in the room."

"With me," Steve groaned, "tipping him off that you had discovered the name of the murderer, and were going to wait around in that dark garden until I showed up at nine o'clock! I ought to get a flock of Carnegie medals, for that!"

"You couldn't know," Ann said softly, "and anyway, you did arrive in time . . ."

"Just luck!" Steve snapped.

"No." The Inspector shook his head. "He was so worried about you, Miss Vickery, all through our drive out, he couldn't talk. I'm the one who should have tumbled to the doctor's little game, long before; it was my job . . ."

"Just what *was* his game?" Senator Kirby growled. "You say he's confessed. Why should a man like that take to murdering people?"

"Dr. Badouine hadn't any idea of committing murder," the Inspector interrupted, "when he started out. Here's his story. Expensive tastes . . . a small income. Six or eight thousand, at the outside. One of the most expensive things he wanted was Mrs. Conover. She was to divorce her husband so they could be married. Her idea seems to have been that they would go to Paris together; get the divorce, then start a long Continental honeymoon. You can't do that on conversation and kisses; the doctor figured he'd need jack. A lot of jack.

"How to get it? Well, poor Mrs. Kirby had plenty and he'd been psycho-analyzing for her for a year, knew all her intimate secrets. Among others, that she had imagined herself, for a time at least, in love with Count de Zara."

The Count turned crimson, but Jean still held his hand.

"An affair *pour passer le temps,*" he muttered. "Not serious. The poor lady, in Cannes, was lonely, bored. I amused her, no more. As a souvenir of an innocent flirtation she wrote an indiscreet message on a snapshot, *'Toujours';* it meant nothing at all."

"When Mrs. Kirby found out," the Inspector went on, frowning, "that the Count, who had come to this country, wanted to marry her daughter she objected: Vanity . . . what not . . . her reasons don't matter now. The important thing is that she told Dr. Badouine, during one of their psyching sessions, about the picture, was terribly worried, for fear the Count might make use of it, to force her consent to the marriage. Mentioned the fact that he kept all his letters and other souvenirs in a certain steel box."

"So that's how he knew!" Steve said.

"Yes. When the doctor heard it, he planned to get hold of the picture. It was simple enough, to ask the Count to show his Napoleon letter . . . figuring he'd leave the box open for a while . . ."

"I do not," de Zara muttered indignantly, "expect guests in my house to steal!"

"Sure." The Inspector agreed. "That's the way Dr. Badouine figured it. And Dane saw him make the pinch."

"That was a bad break for Dane," Steve said, frowning. "It was. Of course he didn't know what it meant, then. Just somebody lifting a picture. Didn't know, after Mrs. Kirby was killed, even, because I'd kept the fact of the picture being found, out of the newspapers. It was only when you, Mr. Ransom, talked to him that he began to connect the two things up."

The Inspector paused for a time. Nobody spoke, and he presently resumed his story.

"I want to straighten matters out, about Dane," he said. "From all I can learn, he didn't write you, Senator Kirby, or Mrs. Kirby, with any idea of blackmail." Duveen turned to Judge Tyson. "You were wrong, too, Judge, about that. Too quick to read between the lines. All he wanted was to raise money for a permanent stock company here in Washington, with himself as leading man. Just a poor ham actor trying to get along. But to go back to Badouine.

"He now had his story for Mrs. Kirby, with a photograph inscribed in her own handwriting to back it up. Something he could sell, for cash. And since he couldn't do the negotiating himself, and was afraid to trust a third party, he framed up the character of a Frenchwoman, a Madame Cardon, who claimed to have been at Cannes at the time and knew the whole works. Wrote Mrs. Kirby, in that name, demanding money. And Mrs. Kirby goes to the doctor and tells him about it, consults him, with the result that he advises her, for the sake of her health and nerves, to pay.

"That's why she had the bonds in her wall safe, all ready to turn over, in exchange for the picture, and a promise on the part of the phony Madame Cardon to go back to France and stay there . . . one of the few promises, I guess, that the doctor really meant to keep. He was going to France, all right, with Mrs. Conover.

"Well, the engagement was made, for Madame Cardon to come and collect, bringing the picture. On a night when the family were all out and the servants and Miss Vickery had been sent off to bed. It was easy, for Badouine, with his slim figure, his dark eyes, to make up as a Frenchwoman. He'd played woman's parts in college theatricals, he tells me, and still had some of the stuff he used, left in a trunk. He dressed in the garage . . . in his car . . . didn't change anything but his shoes and socks. See what I mean? Trousers rolled, pinned up, skirt, long woman's coat, put on over them . . . a soft scarf around his neck . . . a wig . . . small velvet toque. When he got home, driving in the backway, all he had to do was take off a few things, put 'em in his little satchel and walk into the house . . . very neat.

"Everything was jake, Mrs. Kirby got the picture, swung back the china medallion to open the wall safe, and just then the doctor happened to put up a hand to straighten his toque . . . and Mrs. Kirby saw that crooked fingernail. It wasn't as if she'd only seen the thing once or twice before. Dr. Badouine had sat across his desk from her dozens of times and he had a habit of drumming on it with the tips of his fingers. Mrs. Kirby knew that crooked nail as well as she knew her own name and the moment she saw it, she screamed out the fact, grabbed at the doctor's wig!

"That was fatal. He had to stop her, or she would have roused the house. By one of those mistakes that crooks so often make, he'd forgotten completely about his peculiar fingernail. Having had the mark most of his life, he never thought of it as something that might give him away. So he choked Mrs. Kirby, and afterwards killed her, so she couldn't talk, and expose him. Drove the sharp metal penholder into her spine . . . for a man who had studied medicine that was simple; he knew just where to find the vital spot. During the short struggle Mrs. Kirby's necklace was broken. Badouine picked up the pearls, all but the one he accidentally missed, thinking they were real. Put them in his pocket, congratulating himself that even if he hadn't got the bonds, couldn't open the safe to get them, he was almost as well off, having the necklace. He'd already switched on the radio to cover any noises he might make, pushed forward the hands of the clock to make it strike twelve, thinking that if anyone *had* happened to hear Mrs. Kirby call out, they would swear she had been alive at twelve o'clock . . . at which hour he was back at his house, talking to his Negro servant about the message that had just come in over the phone, calling him here. He'd left his car in the lane of course . . . it was seen there . . . a grey sedan, not unlike Mr. Ransom's."

"Clever, damned clever," Senator Kirby muttered.

"He was smart, all right . . . even to changing his voice, putting on a heavy French accent, to deceive Mrs. Kirby. But he made some mistakes, as I've already said. Turning on the radio was one of them; the song on the program proved the clock a liar when it struck twelve . . . thanks to Miss Vickery's sharp ears. Still, his mistakes weren't serious ones. We, the police, hadn't a thing on him . . . nothing at all to connect him with Mrs. Kirby's murder, or even suspect him of it. And next day he did a clever thing. Having discovered, overnight, that the pearls were not real, that he'd come away with a bunch of imitations, he had the nerve to bring them back here, using as an excuse a professional call on Miss Kirby, and when no one was around, dumped them in that flower vase! His idea, he claims, was to throw suspicion on someone in the house, which it did. Just as leaving behind him the now useless snapshot was to throw suspicion on Count de Zara, or Senator Kirby. Quick thinking, believe me. Personally, watching the man as he made his confession, I think he is a little insane. Doctors who treat mental cases sometimes get that way, they tell me. Anyhow, he fooled us completely. Even last night, we hadn't any real evidence against him, wouldn't have had, if Mr. Ransom hadn't taken the law in his hands and, on a chance, opened his medical bag, found his disguise. Once he'd destroyed that, he could have laughed at us. I wonder he didn't, before, but I suppose he thought himself safe, and might need the things again, later."

"How," Ann said, "did he kill Lawrence Dane, and get away with it?"

"That," Duveen replied, "was even more clever. First, he went to the theatre, wearing his woman's disguise, around nine-thirty, at a time when he knew Dane would be on stage. He had the little vial of aconitine in a purse he carried, and a bottle of Scotch whiskey, already opened, under his coat. It took him only a moment to poison the bottle Dane had been drinking from. The fresh one he hid in a corner. Then he drove home, only five or six minutes from the theatre, took off his disguise, came back again in time to meet Mr. Ransom in the lobby at ten. But figure the cleverness of the man . . . that's one reason I think he is insane. He brought that empty poison vial with him, watched Mr. Ransom get out of his car, go into the lobby, and then *planted* the empty vial in the dashboard compartment, stuck into one of Miss Vickery's gloves."

"You say he brought the bottle of White Label Scotch with him on his first visit?" Steve asked.

"Yes. That was sheer genius. As soon as the two of you found Dane lying dead, the doctor sent you out of the room to call the police. Then he took the fresh bottle from where he'd hidden it, poured out enough of the liquor to make it correspond with the poisoned bottle, made the switch. The poisoned whiskey went down the sink . . . the wash basin . . . and the empty bottle went into Dane's wardrobe, along with a lot of other empties. No one would notice another dead one . . . Dane drank a fifth of Scotch a day. And that little device made it unnecessary for the doctor to carry an empty bottle away with him, which might have been dangerous, if anyone had happened to notice the bulge under his coat. The whole scheme was fool-proof . . . perfect . . . except for the matter of the cork."

"How did he know, in advance," Judge Tyson asked, "the brand of Scotch Dane drank? He must have known that."

"I'm afraid," Steve said gloomily, "that I told him. Sometimes I think I talk too much."

"Don't blame yourself, Mr. Ransom," Duveen said. "No trouble to find out. Dane, as a matter of fact, told the doctor at de Zara's studio party that night how he always drank White Label Scotch . . . he was nuts about it."

"And why did Dr. Badouine feel it necessary to kill him?" the Senator asked.

"Because he realized, from what Mr. Ransom told him, that Dane had seen him steal the photograph that night . . . and would say so the moment he was arrested and questioned. The doctor's number would have been up, then. No chance for an out, with that picture found under the dead woman's head.

"The worst feature of the doctor's position, as soon as he found out that Mrs. Kirby's cry of recognition had been heard, was his damaged fingernail. That had him stumped. To have attempted to remove, amputate it would have been worse than useless since any number of persons must have seen the disfigurement, in the past . . . could testify to it. Such an attempt would only have drawn attention to the fact. So he had to fall back on the pretense of assisting Mr. Ransom, the police, in our investigations. Fed us false clues, such as arguing Mrs. Kirby must have said 'Blackmail.' Even asserting, at the end, that you, Senator Kirby, had made homicidal attacks on your wife."

"Scoundrel!" Kirby growled. "I never liked him."

"A smart one, though," Duveen said, "too smart, I guess, for his own good. This morning, down at Headquarters, I got him to put on that disguise for us . . . had him photographed. He didn't mind a bit . . . seemed rather proud of it . . . a nut, all right. Would you believe me, using that assumed voice, a French accent, I wouldn't have known him, right there in broad daylight, let alone night! Perfect! A smart guy!"

Steve turned from the window.

"He gave himself away to me once," he said, "but I was too dumb to realize it. That night at the theatre. He'd told me he had never seen the play before. But when I began to explain the climax of the second act to him, he said 'I know.' He couldn't have known, unless he'd seen the show before, and of course he must have seen it, to be sure Dane would be on the stage, and not in the dressing room, when he went to poison his liquor during the second act. Last night, as soon as Miss Vickery said what she did about a crooked fingernail, I remembered having sat across from Dr. Badouine for an hour, once, in his office, watching him drum on his desk with his finger tips, and that one of his nails was deformed. So I thought if we drove to his house at once, we might catch him with that disguise in his possession."

"It was great work, son!" The Inspector grinned. "We were only just in time, though. Luckily for us, the doctor wasted fifteen minutes driving around back alleys to be sure he wasn't being tailed. And of course he had to stop awhile in his garage to remove the disguise and make-up."

Senator Kirby put out his hand.

"I, too, young man," he muttered, "am profoundly grateful . . . urrrhm . . . keeping my name out of the newspapers . . . as a member of the United States Senate . . . urrhm . . ."

"Don't mention it," Steve said, smiling broadly.

"And," the Senator went on, frowning at the interruption, "if I may offer you gentlemen some refreshment, come along to my study . . ."

"You'll have to go anyway, now," the nurse said, adjusting Ann's pillows. "Dr. Hall gave her only half an hour."

Steve winked at the nurse, waited until the others had left the room.

"Angel!" he whispered.

"No wings and harp yet, thank you!" Ann laughed back.

"Will you be my secretary?"

"I will not!"

"Collaborator?"

"Never! Much too exciting."

"Inspiration?"

"Not in my line."

"Can't we work together in any capacity?"

"Why not? I'm an interior decorator. How about the stage sets for your next play?"

"Fair enough. Take a note, please, Miss Vickery. Act I, Scene I . . . Living Room in the Ransom's Charming Bungalow on Long Island. Up Center, Large Open Fireplace, with Easy Chairs Right and Left. Practical Log Fire . . . Table with Books . . ."

"Time for your medicine, miss," the nurse said.

"I thought it was." Ann grinned up into Steve's face. "Kiss me." It was a long kiss. "We're around that corner now."

Essential! Terribly so! Painfully . . .

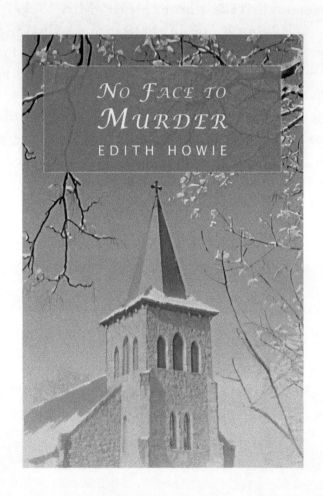

Details at
CoachwhipBooks.com

Available from your favorite online retailers

Details at
CoachwhipBooks.com

Available from your favorite online retailers

The
MURDERS AT HILLSIDE

VIRGINIA RATH

Details at
CoachwhipBooks.com

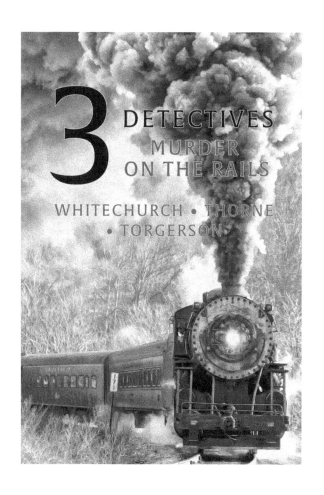

Details at
CoachwhipBooks.com

Available from your favorite online retailers

NARROW
GAUGE TO
MURDER

CAROLYN THOMAS

Details at
CoachwhipBooks.com

Available from your favorite online retailers

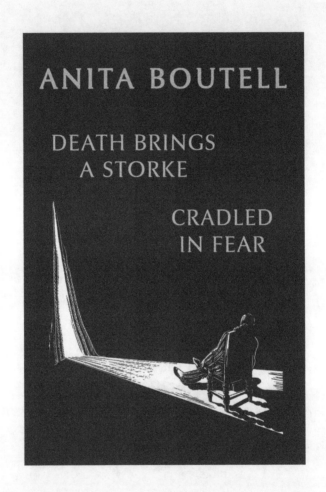

The Adventures of the
Brave Baron von Kaz
in the Northern States of America

1 THE TICKING TERROR MURDERS
THE FEATHER CLOAK MURDERS

DARWIN AND HILDEGARDE TEILHET

Details at
CoachwhipBooks.com

Available from your favorite online retailers

CPSIA information can be obtained
at www.ICGtesting.com
Printed in the USA
BVHW042338060223
658028BV00004B/61

9 781616 465476